# SMOKESCREEN

**Toni Rocha**

# DEDICATION

This book is dedicated to the memory of Shirley White and all those who strive to keep their communities connected with weekly newspapers that reflect their unique characters. Shirley was a walking community historian who taught me the elements of journalism when I first worked as a newspaper reporter for the North Suburban Herald in Rockton, Illinois. I am in her debt.

# TABLE OF CONTENTS

DEDICATION ................................................................ 2

CHAPTER 1 ................................................................... 5

CHAPTER 2 ................................................................. 23

CHAPTER 3 ................................................................. 40

CHAPTER 4 ................................................................. 57

CHAPTER 5 ................................................................. 72

CHAPTER 6 ................................................................. 89

CHAPTER 7 ............................................................... 103

CHAPTER 8 ............................................................... 117

CHAPTER 9 ............................................................... 131

CHAPTER 10 ............................................................. 144

CHAPTER 11 ............................................................. 155

CHAPTER 12 ............................................................. 169

CHAPTER 13 ............................................................. 182

CHAPTER 14 ............................................................. 192

CHAPTER 15 ............................................................. 201

CHAPTER 16 ............................................................. 205

CHAPTER 17 ............................................................... 211

CHAPTER 18 ............................................................... 218

CHAPTER 19 ............................................................... 225

CHAPTER 20 ............................................................... 233

# CHAPTER 1

Ellie Franklin awoke before dawn that Wednesday morning, acutely aware of being totally alone for the first time in her life. On Monday, she had buried Jerry, her husband of more than 32 years. Yesterday, her two sons, daughter and grandchildren had returned to their homes. The house felt too empty. The ticking of the little German cuckoo clock on the wall over her dresser sounded too loud. Ellie pulled the covers more tightly around her and stared up at the ceiling where shadows cast delicate, lacy patterns.

The old adage "Today is the first day of the rest of your life" popped into her head for some weird reason, Ellie nearly burst out laughing. Widowhood felt more like preparing for an extended vacation. Ellie might be moving into new territory, but she suspected she would be taking a lot of baggage along on the journey.

Resolutely, she got out of bed despite the time, a few minutes past 5 a.m. After putting on slippers and pulling a warm robe over her nightgown, Ellie made the bed as she always did before going downstairs to start the day. She padded along the dim hallway past dark, empty bedrooms. Downstairs in the kitchen, Ellie started a pot of coffee. Reaching for one of the printed notepads she always kept on the kitchen counter, Ellie made a note: (1) Buy a smaller coffeepot or maybe a Keurig.

As the aroma of freshly brewing coffee filled the room, Ellie lit candles on the kitchen table and counter. Candlelight in the morning was a tradition she and Jerry had started one wintry January morning in the afterglow of a particularly wonderful Christmas. The soft light dispelled the gloom, as did the comforting sense of routine. The candle lighting was observed through every season, even when sunlight streamed in through the kitchen windows on summer mornings. Carrying her steaming mug of coffee flavored with cinnamon vanilla creamer, Ellie sat down in her usual place at the small oak kitchen table with its inlaid floral ceramic tiles and gazed out of the window at the newly fallen snow.

"Okay, so what am I supposed to do now?" she thought. Again, routine came to her rescue. Normally, she and Jerry would have shared their first cup of coffee and read from a small book of daily meditations. Then they would have discussed what plans they had for the day.

With no one to talk over the day's activities, Ellie read the daily meditation to herself and prayed for guidance for the days to come. "Lord, show me the way for I am in dire need of direction," she whispered.

In place of talking over what the day would bring, Ellie reached for the note pad and began writing: (2) Wash towels; (3) dust mop floors; (4) buy thank you notes; (5) buy stamps; (6) place ad for Jerry's truck. Ellie thought for a moment, then added, (7) look for a part time job, (8) stock up on yarn, and (9) return dishes to neighbors.

Ellie was not the least bit absent-minded or forgetful. Making notes helped organize her day. Besides, she felt personal satisfaction when she checked off completed tasks. Her habit had been a long-standing joke with Jerry, who often had started a comment with, "Ellie, make a note." She liked the colorful printed note pads so much that she bought one or two whenever and wherever she found them. And she saved those that were included in charity requests. The result was a prodigious stockpile in one of the kitchen drawers that would probably supply her note-making needs for several years.

Satisfied with her start to the day, Ellie thought about breakfast. Both she and Jerry had been breakfast eaters. Oatmeal was one of the first things Ellie had learned to cook as a teen, and it remained a comfort food for her. She took the smallest enamel saucepan from the cupboard under the countertop stove. Into it, she measured one-third-cup oatmeal, one-third cup milk and one-third-cup water. Adding a scant teaspoon of wheat germ, a pinch of cinnamon and a handful of raisins, Ellie started the oatmeal cooking over a low flame while she poured a small glass of orange juice and toasted a single piece of bread. Ellie debated eating the oatmeal from the pan instead of dirtying a bowl.

"I am a widow, not an orphan," Ellie sternly scolded herself. "Besides, that is what dishwashers are for." The odd thought occurred that she would now probably run the dishwasher twice a week instead of three or four times, if at all.

She carried the bowl of oatmeal to her seat at the table and ate slowly, relishing the comfort it gave. As she ate, Ellie realized she now had no one but herself to cook for, a depressing thought because Ellie loved to cook. From early childhood, Ellie's mother had encouraged her kitchen skills. Ellie's favorite memories were of Sunday afternoons spent with her mother baking breads, cookies, cakes and pies while soups or stews simmered on the stove. Her family had thrived on meatloaf, pot roast and all those hearty, old-fashioned foods that fed more than just bellies. The phone rang, startling her.

"Good morning, Ellie. Just thought I'd call to see how you are feeling," said the cheery voice of Ellie's closest friend, Janelle Riorson.

"Not all that wonderful."

"I know it's not going to be easy," Janelle said in a matter-of-fact tone. "Anything in particular or everything in general?"

Ellie felt as if she were whining when she answered, "I just realized I no longer have anyone to cook for."

"Nonsense. First of all, Ellie May, you are someone," Janelle replied, using the comic name from the Beverly Hillbillies that nearly always made Ellie smile. "Second, that's why freezers were invented. And third, if you get into cooking mode, you can always send the leftovers here. You know Don and I will eat anything you cook."

At that, Ellie did smile. Everyone deserved a friend like Janelle, Ellie thought, and not for the first time. Janelle and Don Riorson had moved to the small, south central Wisconsin community of Creekwood 18 years ago, and they became close friends right away. Their friendship had grown deeper through the years, due in part to Janelle's marvelous sense of humor and upbeat attitude. Janelle's lack of enthusiasm for cooking had become a long-running joke between them. Janelle's attitude was that, if God had wanted her to cook, He wouldn't have invented restaurants.

"I'll put your names at the top of the list," Ellie quipped, making Janelle chuckle.

"So, what's on that infamous list for today?"

"Housework and returning the dishes people left, including you," Ellie said. "Then I want to sell Jerry's truck so I guess I'll put a classified ad in the Creekwood Courier."

"Good luck with that. And then?"

"Well, I thought I might look for a part time job," Ellie ventured.

"Good," was Janelle's surprising response. "No point in sitting around dwelling on things. Are you going back to the school district?"

"Not if I find something different," Ellie said. "I spent more than 20 years working in that elementary school office. Right now, I feel that I want to try something totally different."

"Like what?"

"I don't have a clue."

"Careful, Ellie. You know what they say about idle hands."

"I thought that was idle minds."

"Those, too."

The women shared a moment of gentle laughter.

"Talk to you later," Ellie said as they ended the call.

Ellie loaded towels in the washing machine, then dust-mopped the kitchen and back door entryway. Thinking about the ad reminded her that she had not yet brought in the weekly edition of the Creekwood Courier. With all of the casseroles and cake pans bagged for return, Ellie sat down at the table for a last mug of coffee and skimmed through the paper. Minutes later, she slapped the newspaper down on the table with a groan of disgust.

"How in the world could anyone make a mistake like that?" Ellie fumed.

Grabbing her note pad, Ellie wrote: (11) Talk to editor about errors. Jerry had shared her frustration at the ineptitude of the Creekwood Courier's social reporting for years. But Jerry had always said to leave be, that no one was perfect and certainly not reporters who tended to work in Creekwood for less than a year before moving on to bigger communities, and more widely read newspapers.

"Well," Ellie thought, "this is one thing I am going to change. I refuse to ignore blatant mistakes such as this ever again."

The problem was that, not only had Ellie and Jerry lived in Creekwood for 31 years, but they had also held positions that constantly put them in contact with nearly everyone else living there. While Ellie had worked in the attendance office at Creekwood Elementary, Jerry had owned the village's only barber shop and worked a chair for 30 years. Ellie had been amazed to learn that men were worse gossips than women. Between them, Ellie and Jerry knew more about the residents of Creekwood and its surrounding neighborhoods than anyone could have possibly imagined. Discretion and respect had prevented them from pointing out many of the Creekwood Courier's errors, because to do so would have revealed things best left unpublished. But this last travesty was more than she could bear.

Showered and dressed in navy slacks and a cream-colored cable sweater, Ellie quickly finished delivering all but Janelle's dishes to neighbors and friends who had brought food when Jerry died. Then she turned onto Main Street and headed west into the downtown district, which was basically four blocks long, neatly divided in half by the intersection of Main Street and Blackthorn Road. Two commercial blocks stretched along East Main and another two along West Main, although only Creekwood's post office ever designated Main Street as east or west. Newer residents said Main Street; long-time residents just said Main. Everyone knew where every single shop, café and office stood along Main, as well as the newer businesses locating north and south of Main along Blackthorn Road.

Just off the southeast edge of the downtown district lay Founder's Park, a pastoral meadow spread along both banks of the Elderberry River which, frankly, was not much bigger than your average creek. Nearly a century before, residents had dammed the river and hand-dug a pond, lining its shores with rounded granite stones. Graceful old oak, clump birch, pine and maple trees were scattered through the park's gently rolling grounds, the historic source of the village's name _ Creekwood.

Historically speaking, the area that would become Creekwood was homesteaded by a gentleman farmer in the mid-1840s, somewhat later than larger neighboring communities that had been established along railroad lines. Because the railroad expansion westward had bypassed Creekwood, the village had grown slowly and changed even more slowly through the decades. Downtown Creekwood, along with most of the original residential development, remained elegantly old-fashioned. The streets surrounding Creekwood's downtown were lined with vintage homes, picket fences and well-established gardens. Ellie often felt as if she were drifting back in time whenever she went downtown to shop or run errands.

Ellie drove past the park, which resembled a Christmas card illustration in black and white on this winter morning. She continued down Main with its angle parking designed to allow as many shoppers as possible access to Creekwood's antique shops, galleries, salons, cafes and craft stores tucked into buildings which were either old or older, easily recognized by their dressed limestone and wood plank facades.

Newer businesses with larger, modern buildings had located along Blackthorn Road. The Creekwood Historical Society had always been nearly beligerent in their insistence that the village's core never be altered, an ongoing campaign that drove the village board crazy on occasion, and sometimes drove new businesses away. Privately, Ellie frequently referred to it as the hysterical society.

Referring to her list, Ellie parked close to CrossEyed & Clueless, a popular shop operated by sisters Nancy and Sonja Pederson. CrossEyed & Clueless featured cross-stitch and other needlework materials combined with a bookshop that sold mostly popular and classic mysteries. CrossEyed & Clueless had expanded rapidly from its original small storefront, and now occupied three storefront spaces along Main. Its merchandise had expanded as well to include all sorts of needlework supplies and picture frames, as well as candles, stationery, gourmet coffees and teas, tin canisters and boxes, and other wonderful stuff.

"Well, good morning, Ellie. What a wonderful surprise," Nancy called from behind the checkout counter. "Come try our sample coffee. It's chocolate raspberry trifle and absolutely decadent."

Ellie accepted a small paper sampler cup and took a sip. She decided immediately that Nancy was right, the coffee was delicious. Jerry had not cared for flavored coffee, so she had seldom had any around the house. Now with only her tastes to satisfy, Ellie decided a package of the fragrant coffee was definitely going home with her.

"So what brings you in?"

"I'm looking for thank you notes, something simple and more on the formal side." Ellie answered.

"Right," Nancy replied as she pulled open one of the storage drawers under a stationery display. "Ellie, I know I've said it before, but I want you to know how sad we all are about your loss."

Nancy and Ellie rummaged through boxes of notes, finding two with the same design that were suited to the occasion. Ellie paid for her purchases, then said goodbye to Nancy and hello to Sonja who came into the store as Ellie left. Leaving the bag in her car, Ellie walked half a block to the post office.

Creekwood's post office occupied the first floor of a 110-year-old limestone two-story building that had once housed a general store. Its postmaster, Helen Lipton, had never married and lived in a tiny apartment above the post office for more years than most Creekwood residents could recall. Elderly and opinionated, Helen had a soft spot for stray animals, especially cats. Ellie knew Helen fed several feral cats from the back stoop on the alley every day.

"Good morning, Helen," Ellie called as she approached the counter. "And good morning to you, too, Postal."

Postal was the official post office pet, a large gray tabby with golden eyes that greeted customers with regal indifference from its usual perch at one end of the counter. Postal had decided to make the post office home years before, sneaking into the building and refusing to be removed without a hissy fit. In fact, the first time Helen had tried to put Postal out, the then unnamed stray had hissed, clawed and bit both Helen and the unfortunate customer who tried to help. Behind her prim and proper demeanor, Helen hid a deliciously wicked sense of humor, hence the cat's name. Helen would find Postal waiting on the wide front porch when she descended the external stairs from her apartment to open the post office at 8:00 a.m. sharp every morning except Sunday. Postal did not desert her post until Helen closed at 5:00 p.m. sharp. Where Postal spent her evenings and Sundays was anyone's guess.

"Good morning, Mrs. Franklin," Helen responded, always formal when performing her duties. "How can I be of service?"

"I need 50 first-class stamps, something sort of staid and proper," Ellie said.

Helen found what Ellie wanted, then uncharacteristically added, "You know that Creekwood just won't be the same without your Jerry. He was always such a gentleman."

"Well, thank you for that, Helen," Ellie replied, tears welling in her eyes at the unexpected kindness.

"That's okay, dear," Helen said, patting Ellie's hand. "I want to you to know he will be missed."

Back in her car, Ellie found a hankie to wipe the tears from her eyes. She tucked the stamps into the bag with the stationery and coffee, then backed out of the parking space and continued west on Main toward the newspaper office.

The Creekwood Courier was headquartered in a one-story free-standing building on a curve at the western end of the village's downtown district. Once a small green grocery, the cream brick building featured wide front windows capped by blue and white striped awnings which allowed the receptionist and editor a commanding view down the entire length of Main. Ellie angle-parked in front and entered through the central glass door. On her right sat the receptionist, Martha Thomas, who Ellie knew because they attended the same church. To her left was a small sitting area and wall with the door to the editor's private office. Beyond Martha and a chest-high wall of filing cabinets, Ellie could see rows of desks arranged along the walls of the building. Some were empty, others were occupied with people talking on telephones or typing on computer keyboards. A low hum of activity and the aroma of fresh coffee permeated the building.

"Well hello, Ellie," said Martha, coming around her desk give Ellie a brief, warm hug. "I'm so sorry about Jerry." At Ellie's brief nod, Martha continued, "How can I help you?"

"I want to place a classified ad for Jerry's truck," Ellie said.

"I can help you with that," Martha replied. She pulled a form from a desk drawer and, for the next 10 minutes, filled in the details for the ad. Ellie paid for a three-week run, then asked if the editor was available.

"Ed's in his office," Martha said. "Let me see if he is free… or at least reasonable," she added with a grin.

Minutes later, Ellie was seated across a cluttered desk from Ed Hathaway, publisher and editor of the Creekwood Courier more than 10 years. Now in his mid-60s, Hathaway was a short, pudgy man with thinning brown hair and clear brown eyes the color of fresh-brewed coffee. Although she had only seen him from time to time around town, and never to talk to, Ellie appreciated the way in which Hathaway focused his full attention on her and was prepared to listen as if to someone he knew well.

"Mr. Hathaway, for years I have refrained from complaining about the errors in your editorial material, but this is the final straw," Ellie began. "On Page 2 in the

Police Blotter, Jackson W. Newell is reported to have been arrested and ticketed for DUI on Friday night."

Ed Hathaway nodded, but said nothing.

"On Page 7 in the Creekwood Social Register, Jackson W. Newell is also reported to be attending a theological seminar with Pastor Ray Johnson in Chicago from Wednesday through Sunday," Ellie added. "The Rev. Jackson W. Newell couldn't possibly have been in two places at once. Furthermore, not only is Rev. Newell a teetotaler but he hasn't owned a driver's license since he turned 80, four years ago."

Hathaway winced visibly and reached for the telephone. Punching in a three-digit extension code, he waited and then quietly stated, "Look at Page 2, column three under the Police Blotter. You see the entry on Jackson W. Newell? Now look at Page 7, column four under Social. You see the entry under Jackson W. Newell? Good. Now, I want you to find out how this mistake was made so it won't happen again. Then, I want you to write a correction for next week's paper. Oh, and if we get telephone calls on this error as I know we will, those calls will all be referred to you so you can explain."

He returned the headphone to its cradle with considerable restraint.

"I need a copy editor…"

"You need a copy editor…"

They stopped talking and just looked at each other. Finally, Ellie smiled self-consciously. The editor leaned back in his chair and tilted his head with a quizzical expression.

"Mr. Hathaway…"

"Call me Ed, please."

He cocked his head to the other side and studied her for a long moment, then abruptly sat upright. "I didn't express my sorrow for your loss, Mrs. Franklin."

"Thank you, and please call me Ellie,"

"Ellie. How long have you lived in Creekwood?"

"Jerry and I moved here around 30 years ago, a bit longer than a year after we were married. He had just finished barbering school and we were starting a family."

"And if I remember correctly, you worked with the school district for a long time, right?"

"That's right. Jerry retired 18 months ago, and I resigned so we could travel and do things together."

They sat through another long moment of silence.

"Things don't always work out the way we want," Ed said with a sigh. "So, what are you going to do now?"

"Oh, I don't know. I haven't thought about it yet, but I believe I should find at least a part time job to help fill the time," Ellie replied. She didn't want to admit to a relative stranger that her finances needed bolstering.

Ed continued to ask pointed questions until Ellie abruptly realized the conversation had started to sound like a job interview. The realization must have shown on her face, because Ed stopped talking. The two stared across the desk at each other again.

"Humph." Ed leaned forward until his forearms were resting on top of the desk. He gazed at her with his direct brown eyes. "You know, your work experience and familiarity with Creekwood makes you an ideal candidate, not only for the copy editing position but also as a social reporter." He hurried on to forestall the denial he saw on her face. "I have reporters for hard news, government, schools and sports but, at this time, I don't have a person capable of writing social features. Most of them don't know the community, and don't take the time to learn. It's one of the reasons why we end up with too many mistakes. Social events are covered by whomever is available. Also, no one seems to have the time to coordinate the stories and items to ensure we don't make stupid mistakes. You could do that."

"Now wait just a minute," Ellie responded. "I know practically nothing about writing."

"But you worked in a school office so you know how to communicate, as well as how to work with people even when they are being difficult. I am positive you know how to operate a computer. Furthermore," Ed said, raising a hand to forestall her protest, "you really know the community and its residents. That's the important thing. We can teach you how to write. It's simply a matter of observing and recording what you see or whom you interview accurately and objectively. Who, what, where, when, why - all the basic elements of reporting, put together with an eye for detail and creative flare."

"It's the creative flare I'm concerned about," Ellie rejoined as a wave of inevitability suddenly washed over her.

"Don't be," he said. "We'll work you into it slowly."

"And if it doesn't work out?"

"I'll accept that with no hard feelings."

Ellie gazed out the window down Main, considering the alternatives. She could possibly find work in one of the village's businesses but that didn't appeal at all. And just what would that entail? Cashiering at one of the gas stations? Filing and answering telephones? Bagging groceries? She had prayed just that morning for direction, and by golly, the good Lord seemed to be answering her prayer, although not at all in the way she had expected.

Her head was spinning with the notion of writing for a newspaper, something she had never even remotely considered. Good grief, she thought, what was it Janelle had said just that morning about idle hands? Or was it minds? A reckless mood came over her and, before she could stop, she heard herself saying, "Okay, I'll give it a try."

"Great! Why don't you plan on coming in Friday morning? We can get you acquainted with our software and start you on the copy editing right away. One of the reporters can mentor you on the basics of writing features."

Ed offered her $12.00 an hour to start, generosity Ellie had not expected as an untrained person. Numbly, she left his office, absent-mindedly said goodbye to Martha and walked to her car. Without thinking clearly, she drove to Janelle's house.

Janelle took one look at Ellie's face, sat her down at the kitchen table and put the kettle on for tea.

"My goodness, Ellie, you look as if you're in shock," Janelle fussed. "What on earth happened since I talked to you this morning?"

"Remember when we were talking about my getting a part time job and I said I didn't know what I was going to do?"

Janelle nodded.

"Now I really don't know what I'm going to do!" Ellie wailed.

# CHAPTER 2

By the time Ellie finished breakfast and blew out the candles Thursday morning, she had another long list of things to do. Reassessing her wardrobe was at the top of the list, but Ellie decided to hold off on that project until evening. Instead, she put a Stephan Grappelli CD in the player, poured a fresh mug of coffee, and began writing thank-you notes.

As she wrote, she realized that one of her biggest fears, loneliness, had so far failed to materialize. Ellie understood the difference between being alone _ something she had always been comfortable with _ and feeling lonely, something she dreaded. One good reason she had not felt lonely so far, she thought ruefully as the stack of finished thank-you notes grew steadily, was the strong network of friends the Franklins had forged through the years they had lived in Creekwood.

Ellie had grown up with loving parents, two sisters and a brother in a house filled with music, laughter and faith. She married Jerry, a man 12 years her senior, when she was 22, moving from one home into another without living on her own. The Franklins had moved to Creekwood. During those early years, Ellie had stayed home to raise their two sons and daughter.

The small home they had bought on Benning Lane had been barely more than a shell. Ellie and Jerry had done most of the remodeling themselves, starting with the kitchen she loved best of all the rooms in the house. Compact and neatly designed, the cooking area occupied half of the room, separated by a counter from a corner dining area that held an oblong, tile-topped table and four chairs. They had enlarged the windows along the south and east walls to let sunlight stream in through lacy curtains.

A small bathroom opened off another wall in the kitchen. Besides the kitchen and bath, the ground floor included a living room with a field stone fireplace, a formal dining room and a small sunroom behind the kitchen with patio doors that opened onto the redwood deck Jerry had built one summer. Upstairs were four small but charming bedrooms and the main bath. Ellie's love of earthy colors pulled the entire home's décor together. From the buttery yellow kitchen, her color scheme included heather-toned browns and tans, bittersweet, forest green, butterscotch and cream on the main floor. Upstairs, each bedroom still reflected her children's personalities, from Susan's dainty rose and white to Jerry Jr.s' sporty red, white and blue, and David's green-brown love of horses.

Ellie's bedroom was a soothing blend of sage green, pale peach and cream. Before the children had left for home Tuesday morning, Ellie had asked her sons to move the king-sized bed she and Jerry had shared to Susan's old room and replace it with Susan's super single. The smaller bed left room for an antique wooden rocker the boys had brought up from the basement. Ellie had already decided she liked the change. Instead of just being a place to sleep and dress, the bedroom now felt more like a retreat. Not that she had anything or anyone from which to retreat, Ellie thought ruefully as she licked the flap on the last note. After all, she had the entire house to herself now.

"Now all I have to do is some creative tucking to make the bed skirt fit," Ellie thought as she dropped the notes into the mailbox by the front door so Mike Jensen, the village mailman, would pick them up. "I can paint Susan's white backboard and the rocker cream to match the decor."

Upstairs, Ellie tackled the next job on her list, packing Jerry's clothes for the Creekwood Methodist Church's thrift shop. Creekwood was such a small community that its churches divided charitable efforts between them rather than compete. Thus, thrift shop donations went to the Methodists while Ellie's church, Creekwood Community, operated a modest food pantry. Creekwood Congregational used monetary donations to help local families who had suffered setbacks or disasters.

As she pulled shirts and slacks from the closet and folded them neatly into stacks on the bed, Ellie couldn't help but contrast this January with the last one. One year ago, we were packing for the cruise, Ellie mused. Six months ago, we were up by Hayward on the fishing trip Jerry had always talked about taking. Thinking back, Ellie realized that subtle symptoms of Jerry's illness were already manifesting. He had tired so easily. Why didn't we sense something was wrong, Ellie wondered as she pulled clothing from drawers and began filling boxes. One month ago, we were praying Jerry would make it through the holidays. A week ago, he died. Dear Lord, what am I going to do with the rest of my life?

Her reverie was interrupted by the familiar clank of the lid dropping on the mailbox. Ellie went downstairs and grabbed a slim stack of envelopes from the box. Carrying the mail, she went back to the kitchen. Sure enough, among the cards and letters was the one envelope she dreaded opening _ the bill from the University of Wisconsin-Madison Hospital where Jerry had spent the last few days of his life. Might as well get it over with, she murmured as she tore open the envelope.

"It's not as bad as I thought. It's worse."

The figures swam before Ellie's eyes as they teared up. Jerry had just turned 67 when he had been diagnosed with a particularly aggressive type of cancer that past October. Ellie knew that the total on this bill did not take into consideration any payments made by Medicare and the supplemental insurance Jerry had carried. Still, whatever remained to be paid might possibly take an enormous chunk of their savings. Sinking slowly into a chair at the kitchen table, Ellie cupped her head in her hands, letting grief and fear wash over her. Ellie could do nothing to stop the torrent of good and bad memories that followed.

Jerry had sold the barbershop business and building to one of his employees shortly after he retired at 65. With Jerry's Social Security, interest on the investments from the sale and her state pension, Jerry and Ellie had been positioned to live frugally but comfortably. The house, Ellie's car and Jerry's truck were paid off, thank goodness. They had taken money out of savings for an extravagant 10-day Hawaiian cruise, something Ellie refused to begrudge because of the joy it had given them.

At 55, Ellie was too young for Social Security or Medicare. With medical and house and car insurance, property taxes, utilities, and all those other expenses, the interest alone would not cover everyday expenses, never mind major medical bills. On those long nights when Jerry slept fitfully and she not at all, Ellie had considered selling the house. In the end, she decided she would stay. Rent might cost more than the total taxes, insurance and upkeep on the house. The prospect of moving after 30 years had influenced her decision as well. Ellie would have had to give up too many things she loved. And where would the children and grandchildren stay when they came to visit?

"Well, hopefully Jerry's truck will fetch a decent price. Thank God I've already found a job," Ellie told herself.

Ellie ate one of her favorite lunches, thin shaved ham on buttered toast with a sprinkle of pepper. Then she rinsed the navy beans she had soaked overnight in her blue granite soup pot. She added frozen homemade chicken broth, water and the ham bone from Christmas dinner, then put the soup to simmer at the back of the stove.

Down in the basement, Ellie rummaged through the storage area until she found quart and pint canning jars with lids. Upstairs again, Ellie washed the jars and set them on the counter beside the stove. Outside the kitchen window, the day had darkened into heavy overcast that looked suspiciously like more snow. Sighing, Ellie thought how comforting it felt to have a pot of soup going on winter days such as this one. Sharing the soup with friends made it even better. Besides, bean soup didn't freeze well in Ellie's opinion; it tended to get grainy and lose a lot of its savor.

She was headed for the stairs to start bringing Jerry's clothing down when the phone rang.

"Ellie, I'm calling to remind you that our regular meeting of the Federated Woman's Club is tomorrow morning," Ginny Henderson said.

"Boy, am I glad you called," Ellie replied. "I had completely forgotten."

"That's understandable."

"And worse, I can't be there," Ellie said, then debated for only a second before adding, "I am starting a part-time job at the Creekwood Courier tomorrow morning."

The silence at the other end was palpable.

"My goodness, Ellie, that is, ummmm, interesting," Ginny said tentatively "How ummmm, different. What are you going to do there?"

Good question, Ellie said to herself. To Ginny, she said, "To start, I guess I am going to type all the public service announcements, coordinate information and edit copy.

Later on, Ed Hathaway seems to believe I will actually cover and write up social events."

"How in the world did you ever get that job," Ginny gasped, then quickly backtracked. "I mean, not that I don't think you'll do a good job. Especially when it comes to helping avoid those ghastly mistakes the Courier makes. But you have no experience with this kind of work... or do you?"

"None at all, but I have always sort of wanted to write something," Ellie answered. "As to how I got the job, I went in to complain about that horrible error the Courier printed about Rev. Newell. And, you know how they always say the squeaking wheel gets the grease?"

"Yes?" Ginny prompted.

"Well, I squeaked and got hired."

"Oh, brother. Were you looking for work?"

"I just can't see me sitting around the house doing nothing," Ellie temporized. Her financial situation was no one's business, most certainly not in small-town Creekwood. "On the other hand, the usual jobs available in Creekwood don't appeal to me much."

"Well, we are going to miss you tomorrow. Unless, of course, you start covering our meetings?" Ginny said hopefully. "Anyway, good luck. Knowing you, Ellie, I just know you are going to be a huge asset to the Courier. I have always believed you to be one of the most capable people I know."

"Thank you for your vote of confidence, Ginny."

"You're very welcome. And I will be sure to pass on the good new that you're going to be in charge at the Courier. Bye, Ellie." Ginny ended the call before Ellie could correct her.

Good grief, Ellie thought as she hung up. How could Ginny have misconstrued Ellie's new position so completely? Now the news would be all over town, most likely before she went to church on Sunday. With Martha Thomas working as Courier receptionist, the news was probably common knowledge throughout most of Creekwood already. As in any other small community, the Creekwood grapevine was healthy and well watered.

Shrugging off her concerns, Ellie finished carrying Jerry's clothes from the bedroom downstairs to the garage door where she could easily put them in the car trunk. She stirred the soup and began assembling the ingredients for honey cornbread. While the rich aromas of simmering soup and baking bread filled the kitchen, Ellie diced carrots, potatoes, celery and onion to add to the soup pot along with sweet basil, parsley, minced garlic and black pepper.

This time when the telephone rang, Janelle was on the other end.

"You'll never guess what I just heard," Janelle began.

"Oh, I bet I can. I thought I smelled the aroma of burning telephone lines."

"Um-hum. Ginny called to remind me of tomorrow's meeting and, by the way, to let me know you are taking over the editorial department at the Courier."

Ellie groaned. "I told her I was going to copy edit and type announcements, and maybe write articles in the future. How could she have possibly turned that into a full editorship?"

"Well, no one has ever accused Ginny of lacking imagination," Janelle said, laughing.

"I'm not so sure it's funny," Ellie groused.

"Oh, come on. No one with an ounce of common sense is going to believe that you are single-handedly taking over the Courier, Ellie."

"You know the trouble with common sense? It isn't."

"Common, you mean. But you have to admit, this one is a stretch."

"Yeah, right. And I'll spend the rest of my life trying to live it down."

"Never mind the rest of your life. What are you doing for supper?"

"I took your advice, Janelle. I'm making a pot of bean soup and cornbread. In fact, I was just getting ready to fill a quart jar with soup and cut some cornbread to bring you tomorrow morning before I go to work."

"Bless you, Ellie! I bless you, Don blesses you. We were going to take you out to eat but it sounds as if you have everything well in hand."

"Thank you for the thought," Ellie replied with a smile. "Tonight, I need to go through my clothes and try to decide what to wear to work. I'm trying to remember what the people at the Courier were wearing when I was there yesterday."

"I wouldn't worry about it overly much, especially the first day. I suspect they are fairly casual."

"Martha was wearing a skirt and sweater set, but she's front office," Ellie added. "I will probably be stuck behind a desk and computer screen in the farthest corner. I'm thinking slacks and a warm sweater. Oh, and warm socks. Those older buildings can be drafty."

"Sounds about right to me. So, I'll expect you when, about 8 tomorrow morning?"

"About then. I need to get to the office early and fill out the paperwork before I start working," Ellie replied, suddenly struck by how odd that sounded. *Starting a new career at my age*, she thought.

After exchanging good-byes with Janelle, Ellie ladled soup into the two jars and cut cornbread into squares. She wrapped four pieces to go with Janelle's quart of soup, and two pieces to go with the pint jar. Then she divided the rest of the soup into plastic bowls with lids and put them in the refrigerator along with individually wrapped pieces of cornbread. Putting on a jacket that always hung from a hook under a small wooden shelf by the back door, Ellie took the pint jar and cornbread with her across the yard to her neighbor's house.

Catherine Bradford had been living in the house next door when the Franklins bought their home more than 30 years before. Her husband had passed away years before, and her children had moved away. Now 80-something years of age, Catherine was reclusive and seldom left her home except once a week to attend church and shop. Frequently, Catherine refused to answer the door if she did not know, or want to talk to, the visitor outside.

But Ellie had built a rapport with the older woman through the years. Mostly, they talked whenever they were outdoors working on their yards and gardens. Jerry had removed snow from Catherine's sidewalks whenever he cleared their driveway and walks of snow and ice. Despite their good-neighbor relationship, Ellie had rarely been invited into Catherine's home, and out of sensitivity had never invited herself in. On this cold winter afternoon, however, Ellie knocked on Catherine's kitchen door and hoped she would answer. The door opened a crack, then immediately swung wide open.

"Ellie, what a nice surprise. Come in."

Ellie entered Catherine's kitchen with the same innate sense of ease she always felt during the few times she had visited. The room was farmhouse sized and warmly lit, with a round antique maple table and four chairs in the middle. Along one wall, an enormous woodburning stove like Ellie's grandmother had used radiated heat although it had been converted to gas long ago. Beside and behind it, an open door led to a pantry lined with sturdy wooden shelves and rows of home-canned fruits and vegetables. Two golden loaves of bread sat cooling on a counter that ran the full length of another wall, their fresh-baked aroma lingering. Above the counter, old-fashioned glass-front cabinets showcased an impressive collection of Depression glass in delicate pastel hues. Everything from the creamy lace curtains to the gleaming hardwood floors was immaculately clean, as always.

"I just put the kettle on for tea," Catherine was saying. "Now, what is it you have there?"

Ellie handed the still-warm jar of soup and cornbread to Catherine.

"It seemed the ideal day to make a batch of soup. I wanted to bring some over to share with you," Ellie replied. "Besides, there is no such thing as a small batch of bean soup."

"I know exactly what you mean," Catherine said with a gentle smile, setting them on the counter and reaching for two china teacups on a cupboard shelf. "Besides, good homemade bean soup doesn't freeze well, does it? Would you like orange spice or Earl Grey?"

"Earl Grey is one of my favorites."

"Mine, too," Catherine said. "Please, sit down."

While the looseleaf tea steeped, Catherine arranged cookies on a dainty rose glass plate, then placed a matching sugar and creamer set on the table. After precisely five minutes, she poured tea and sat down across from Ellie with a little sigh.

Catherine began speaking with a directness that startled Ellie. "You are my friend _ you and Jerry, too _ and have been for many years even though it has been a somewhat unconventional relationship. I will miss that dear, sweet man."

Ellie started to say, "I hesitated to intrude."

"You of all people are not intruding, Ellie. I am a simple person and not an adventurous one, I confess," Catherine continued, patting Ellie's hand reassuringly. "I decided to make this house my world long ago, and to be content with my lot in life. This house is me, filled with the things I love and where I spend my time doing the things I love _ cooking, sewing, reading. If there is a better way to live, I don't know about it nor do I miss it at all. Now, drink that tea while it is still hot. Tea is a magic potion that can cure most of the world's ills if properly and faithfully applied."

Ellie laughed outright at that, and felt her initial uneasiness fade away. Within minutes, she was telling Catherine about her new job at the Courier as if they had sat at this table and talked daily for a lifetime. When the time came to go home, Catherine pressed a plate of cookies into Ellie's hands and extracted a promise to keep her posted on how the job was going. Walking across the frosted yard in the twilight, Ellie shook her head and wondered what exactly had just happened between Catherine and herself. It felt as if the long-standing relationship had suddenly shifted into a different gear.

After her own supper of bean soup and cornbread, Ellie went upstairs to face the clothing project that had been at the top of her list. The closet looked so empty. For years, she had stored some of her clothes in Susan's bedroom closet and dresser because there wasn't enough room in the master bedroom. Now there was more than enough space, a fact that threatened to bring tears to Ellie's eyes once again.

Fighting off the urge to cry, Ellie stared into the closet and realized this was going to be one of those chores where, in order to choose what to wear in the morning, she would first need to do about four other things. Oh, well, Ellie thought, it is not as if I had anything else to do tonight.

First Ellie rearranged the dresser next to the closet so that her underwear and hosiery were together in the top drawer. Then she began sorting sweaters and storing them in the next two drawers. Finally, she carried her sweatshirts and jeans from Susan's room to hers and neatly stacked them in the bottom two drawers. Ellie made more trips to Susan's room, returning each time with her arms loaded with dresses, blouses and slacks. The busy work helped. In less than an hour, Ellie had the closet organized to her satisfaction.

Now I have a dressing station if not a dressing room, Ellie told herself. Gazing into the closet, she smiled as something Catherine had said that afternoon came to mind. When Ellie had commented on a collection of Martha Stewart Living magazines in a small wooden rack by the kitchen table. Catherine had wryly admitted to being a "closet Martha Stewart fan."

"She does things with such grace and ease," Catherine had added with a shrug. "I admire that ability."

Now Ellie stood back, studied her newly arranged closet, grinned and murmured, "It's a good thing."

Another possible explanation for Catherine's unexpected hospitality suddenly occurred to Ellie. When Jerry and I first moved here, we must have seemed so much younger than Catherine, Ellie realized. Then we had children when hers were already grown and gone. When our children were grown, we were still a married couple and Catherine was a widow. Now we are equals at last, Ellie thought, and wondered how other relationships might change.

Ellie's cell phone rang and she answered, to find her daughter Susan on the other end.

"So, Mom, how's it going?"

"Okay so far, dear," Ellie replied. "I just finished reorganizing my closet so that all my clothes are in one place now."

"Wow, after how many years?"

"Too many," Ellie said with a small laugh. "Besides, I had to sort through it all to separate work from house outfits."

"Work?" Susan exclaimed. "You got a job? Oh, my goodness, Mother. Are you going back to the school office?"

As Susan listened attentively, Ellie told her all about the visit to the newspaper office and how it had led to getting a part-time job.

"That is absolutely amazing," Susan said, excitedly. "Wait until the boys hear about this. They're going to love it. I do. I can just see you behind a computer, pencil tucked over one ear, phone ringing, deadline approaching, awesome!"

"Oh, I don't know about that," Ellie temporized. "I suspect it will be more in line with finding mistakes, clarifying statements and making certain all the community events get listed properly."

"Don't downplay it, Mom," Susan protested. "You are one of the most capable people I know. You can do this. I want to hear every detail. When do you start?"

"Tomorrow morning. I need to fill out the usual forms and then one of the reporters is going to help orient me."

Ellie assured Susan that she would keep her informed and they said their goodbyes. Ellie gazed around the serene, simply appointed bedroom and sighed. Everyone thinks I will be good at this reporting and copy editing job, she told herself. Now, if I could only believe it myself.

# CHAPTER 3

Entering the Creekwood Courier office the next morning with a sack lunch in hand, Ellie felt like a kid on the first day of school. The winter day was diamond bright and cold. Ellie was glad she had chosen to wear her charcoal gray corduroy slacks with a heavy, red cable-knit sweater.

After she had filled out various employment forms with Martha Thomas, Ellie was given a brief tour of the building by an obviously distracted Ed Hathaway. Aside from the newsroom with its half-dozen desks, Ed showed her the bathroom and employee lounge. Ellie gingerly put her lunch into a refrigerator desperately in need of cleaning. The long, narrow lounge also held two round, scarred chrome tables with four chairs each and a large wooden counter. The enticing aroma of freshly brewed coffee wafted from a commercial coffee maker. Ellie was pleased to note a small microwave on the counter.

"You might want to bring a coffee mug instead of using the foam cups. Most of the others have their own. We did some rearranging for you," Ed told Ellie. "Your desk is the first on the right when you walk into the editorial room. Now that you will be handling the public service announcements, you will need room to talk to people who come in, in person."

Ellie was pleasantly surprised to find her desk was right up in front. She had expected to be relegated to somewhere in the back of the room. Her desk faced an aisle but was set back far enough to allow space for two padded chairs. In addition to the computer monitor and keyboard, the desk held a calendar, dictionary, telephone, stack of reporter's notepads, a stapler, a cup of pens and pencils, and a metal in-basket already piled with unopened envelopes and multi-colored fliers.

"I asked Kirsten Patrick to mentor you," Ed continued. "Kirsten is our hard-news and police reporter as you probably already know, and has the most time in at the Courier. She will answer any questions you have about the computer programs, copy editing and entering information. Any questions about content or concerns you have during editing should be directed first to the reporter who wrote the article, or to me if you are not satisfied with the response."

Ed broke off and, running a hand through his thinning hair, wandered back into his office. Ellie gazed after him, perplexed. Two days ago, Ed Hathaway had impressed her as a calm, strong and well-organized person. Today, he seemed markedly different.

Irrationally, Ellie hoped she was not the cause although she couldn't imagine how or why she would be. She slowly sat down behind her desk and wondered what to do next. Martha came around the file cabinets that separated the reception area from the editorial room and sat down in one of the visitor chairs.

"As far as the PSAs are concerned, that's public service announcements," Martha began in her matter-of-fact manner, "if I know what it is, I'll drop it into your in-box unopened. Sometimes I don't know and then the envelope will be open. I used to put all the PSAs in a basket on top of the file cabinets here. Whenever a reporter had free time, he or she was expected to grab a handful and type them up. I'm relieved that you are going to be working on them exclusively from now on."

Well, that certainly explains a few things, Ellie thought to herself.

Martha went on, "Telephone calls relating to PSAs will be referred to you. And let me warn you, Ellie, some of these organizations are fiercely determined to get their fair share of space and then some. I've even had a few come in with rulers and point out that certain other organizations were given more space."

"You're kidding," Ellie burst out before she could stop. "On second thought, I bet I can guess who they were."

"I bet you can, too, and I wish you joy of them," Martha added dryly. "Kirsten will be in, any minute. She covered the village council meeting last night so she will have that story to write plus any related side issues."

The front door opened, and Martha left to greet whoever had entered. Ellie leaned back in the chair and took a thoughtful look around the editorial room. The walls were covered with dark walnut wainscoting topped with pale gray painted plaster. Large framed color photos of various scenes from the Creekwood community were spaced across the plaster portion, softening the cold, neutral feel of the room. The ceiling was acoustic tile crossed by recessed florescent lighting. The metal desks were uniformly dark gray with black tops, fitted with matching two-drawer file cabinets, black phones and silver metal file baskets. Each had the prerequisite computer and keyboard which, she was happy to note, were Macs. Ellie didn't see printers, which made her curious. A copier and flat-drawer files were located along one wall where the sales person probably had a desk. All in all, a very businesslike atmosphere, Ellie decided.

Ellie was just opening a desk drawer to see what was inside when Kirsten breezed in, coat flapping over a beautiful pale gray sweater that turned her hair redder and eyes greener. Ellie had seen Kirsten around town, of course, but had never spoken to her.

"Hey! You're Ellie Franklin," Kirsten said, slipping her coat off and sliding into the chair at the desk next to Ellie in one smooth movement. "Let's get you started on those dreaded PSAs right away. First, the computers stay on all the time. Are you familiar with Microsoft Word?"

At Ellie's nod, Kirsten looked noticeably relieved. "Good, because it's the word processing program we all use."

Briskly but at the same time patiently, Kirsten instructed Ellie about how to log on and where to find the file folder labeled "Edit" that held articles for copy editing.

One was named "PSA." Well, that's simple enough, Ellie thought.

"Let me give you a brief overview of how the system works," Kirsten was saying. "We write our stories and post them in the "Edit" file folder. You will do the copy editing for each story in the folder and, when you finish, post a copy of the story into the "Publish" file folder. Ed does the final edit, then sends the approved version to Jennifer Stanley, our graphics composer, in the back room. Jennifer formats all articles, photos, columns and ads into finished pages on her computer, then sends them to the printing company in Brodhead. The pages are made into plates that go on the press and, Voila! _ a newspaper is born."

Kirsten told Ellie that, behind the editorial room wall was not only the composing but also the circulation office where a manager and staff of three were responsible for getting the Creekwood Courier out of the door, and into stores and homes throughout the community.

"Any questions so far? No? Okay, about those PSAs," Kirsten said with a huge grin. "Open the PSA file, and you will see what is already entered. Don't worry about format, just type in the information using the style you see already set up."

"Shouldn't they be in some sort of order?"

"Yes, they certainly should although that doesn't always happen," Kirsten agreed. "You need to keep in mind that Ed gives Jennifer what we call dummies, layouts that indicate how much editorial and ad space is allocated for each page. The space allowed for PSAs differs from week to week, depending on whatever else has to get in. Jennifer cuts the PSAs off from the bottom up. Therefore, common sense dictates entering them based on chronological order, first things first."

The slight hint of sarcasm in Kirsten's voice tipped Ellie to one of the reasons why the PSAs weren't always in time-based order.

"Some people seem to feel PSAs should be published in order of what they believe is most important," Kirsten added, confirming Ellie's suspicions. "Just remember, Ellie, you are now in charge of PSAs. Oh, and the deadline for PSAs is noon Monday. No exceptions, no excuses."

"Polite but firm," Ellie replied, "just like we handled parents in the attendance office."

"You got it," Kirsten said, laughing. "You're the boss. When the VOLs come in to complain, you can explain why their event is halfway down the list instead of on top."

"VOLs?"

"Venerable old ladies," Kirsten quipped, nearly causing Ellie to choke. "Now, let's get some fresh coffee and get to work."

Seated at her desk again with a borrowed mug of coffee, Ellie decided her first step would be to eliminate all the out-dated announcements. She methodically went down the list, highlighting and deleting. Then she rearranged the remaining PSAs in strict order, not only for date but also for time. Once that task was finished, Ellie tackled the stack of PSAs in her in-box.

"I have a question."

"Shoot."

"Is it possible to separate PSAs into three different columns? I mean, the events could go on the news pages with the Community-in-Action calendar, while the church activities could go on the church page and the club meetings on the community page."

"First, you would have to clear it with Ed so he can dummy in the space on the pages, then Jennifer must be made aware of the changes," Kirsten replied. Taking a closer look at Ellie's desk, Kirsten added, "Boy, are you organized. One other thing to consider is that three files won't be a problem when we have a 24-page newspaper. But if the paper falls to 20 or 16 pages, it could be more difficult to fit them separately."

Seeing the blank look on Ellie's face, Kirsten picked up a copy of the Courier, spread it across the desk and explained, "See, tab-sized newspapers like the Courier are printed in four-page sheets. The number of pages depends directly on the amount of ad space sold, particularly what we call the 'legals,' then the obits, followed by the advertising and then editorial content. In order to publish legals in the classified, which is a large portion of the paper's revenue, the Courier has to publish more than a minimum number of editorial inches. Otherwise, it would be considered a shopper and not eligible for legal classified ads. It's a weekly juggling act that Ed is an expert on."

"This is a lot more complicated than I imagined," Ellie said, studying the paper thoughtfully.

"Don't worry about those issues. That's Ed's area of expertise. My advice is to ask. Ed is almost always in favor of changes that make the paper more readable. Actually, smaller files are more flexible as a rule."

"And the VOLs will get their announcements closer to the top," Ellie added.

"There's that," Kirsten agreed with a grin. "But wait a while before you ask Ed. Now isn't a good time. But it is a good time to introduce you to Jennifer and the circulation crew"

Kirsten led the way back through the editorial department to a pair of heavy doors that swung open into the rear of the Courier building. Storage and file cabinets lined the right wall all the way to the rear of the building where Ellie could see a garage door. Along the left wall were a series of small offices, all but one with glass windows looking out into what at one time, was the press room.

"Those file cabinets hold all the old issues, the Courier archives, in case we need to look something up from before computer disc storage and microfische. The shelving is where we store office supplies and other stuff. That first room with no window was the darkroom, the second is Jennifer's office and the other offices are circulation."

"Darkroom? Do you still need one with digital photography?" Ellie wondered aloud.

"No," Kirsten responded. "Jennifer used to have a blackbox drawer in her office which went through the wall and into the darkroom. She printed out the full pages after they were composed, then put them into the drawer. The technician pulled them into the darkroom where they were photographed and made into plates. That process has all been replaced when Ed got rid of the press and outsourced the printing."

A petite young woman with long, straight brown hair looked up as they entered the office. Kirsten made the introductions, then waited while Ellie explained what she was thinking of changing.

"The files could be named PSAchurch, PSAevents and PSAclubs," Ellie ended, writing them on a small notepad so Jennifer could see how she spelled them out.

"Sounds okay to me, but we would need to create new headers over the columns," Jennifer pointed out.

"Headers?"

Jennifer opened a Courier to the community pages and pointed to a half-inch deep box with a screened background that said "Community Events" in bold type.

"That."

"Oh, that," Ellie said. "Can I have a little more time to come up with titles?"

"Yup. You have until noon Monday noon," Jennifer said straight-faced.

"No excuses. No exceptions," all three said at the same time, then burst out laughing.

Back once more at her desk, Ellie opened the PSA file, and began typing in the new copy. But after finishing the stack of new notices, she was troubled by something she felt was missing.

"Martha?" Ellie called over the file barrier. "Did you happen to notice if the Methodist Church sent anything in about their annual pie and rag rug sale?"

After a moment's silence, Martha replied, "No, as a matter of fact, I haven't seen one."

Ellie looked over at Kirsten, who responded, "When in doubt, call and ask."

Ellie called the church office, and was referred to Melody Wilson, who had volunteered to chair this year's sale. She was taken aback when Melody's husband, Bruce, answered the call. She was even more startled to learn Melody had fallen on the ice, and broken an ankle several days before.

"Melody is in a lot of pain yet," Bruce continued. "And it is next to impossible to use her desktop computer with a leg propped up on a chair in front of her. Not that Melody hasn't tried. And her two committee members are in Madison at a quilting seminar."

"Can she give me the information over the phone," Ellie asked. "The church has hosted this for what, 27 years? I know everything except this year's hours. If she can talk to me right now, I'll get the announcement in next week's issue."

With the phone's headset clenched between her chin and shoulder, Ellie keyed the sale information directly into the PSA file. After hanging up, she saved the file and sent a copy to Ed.

"Okay, what do I do with these?" Ellie asked Kirsten, holding up the finished stack of announcements.

"Put them in your alibi file."

"My what?"

"Keep them in a file folder in your desk until at least one month after the event."

"Really?"

"You'd be amazed," Kirsten said dryly. "Ready to break for lunch?"

When Ellie told Kirsten she had brought lunch and put it in the refrigerator, Kirsten shuddered delicately.

"I usually order something from the PC," Kirsten said, referring to the Pinecone Café across the street and down half a block. "Today is chicken and dumpling soup day."

When Kirsten left to pick up her lunch, Ellie wandered back to the lounge and took her sack lunch out. Frowning, she studied the refrigerator but refrained from giving in to a strong urge to sweep everything out of it into the nearest garbage can. As Ellie chewed on her ham and Swiss sandwich, Kirsten swept into the lounge with a steaming covered bowl of soup and a spiral bound white book.

"No rest for the wicked, even during lunch," Kirsten quipped. Slapping the book down on the table, she added, "this is the AP style book, otherwise known reverently by the staff as the bible. Ed expects us all to follow this style even if it falls off the Elderberry River bridge."

Ellie flipped through the pages and thoughtfully munched on her sandwich. Unsure if she should ask what could be a sensitive question, she decided she really needed to know.

"Kirsten, is something bothering Mr. Hathaway? Because he acted so differently toward me today than he did Wednesday, I mean," Ellie began.

Kirsten rose from her seat and peered out into the editorial area. Then she came back to the table and leaned close to Ellie.

"This isn't for publication, but Ed's wife had a routine mammogram last week and they found a lump," Kirsten murmured in a low voice. "She is in Madison having a biopsy today and he is understandably upset."

"I can identify with that," Ellie replied.

"So can we all," Kirsten muttered.

After lunch, Ellie began reading through the stories already filed for the next issue, which she learned would be sent to press on Monday night. It amazed her to learn that the paper would be printed, folded and delivered to the circulation staff early Tuesday. The papers would be divided up into routes and given to the delivery people for distribution Wednesday morning. She didn't find too much that seemed wrong in the features, especially those submitted by Kirsten. Ellie focused mostly on grammar and spelling, intuitively guessing that the publisher would be the appropriate one to address content. She did watch for things that might not be accurate or that conflicted with earlier data, but found little she questioned. The afternoon slipped by quickly.

As she put on her coat to leave, Ellie asked Kirsten about the next week's schedule.

"You really don't have to work beyond 1 p.m. on Mondays," Kirsten explained. "On Tuesday afternoon, we have our weekly editorial meeting to determine the next issue's content and receive our assignments. Just come back in at 2 p.m. Tuesday and we'll go from there."

That left the entire weekend with nothing to do except Sunday morning church services. Ellie slid into her car and decided to stop at Crafty Like a Fox to buy the yarn she had noted on her to-do list earlier in the week. Located in a turn-of-the-century brick and gingerbread house on Blackthorn next to the river bridge, Crafty Like a Fox stocked not only a good selection of yarn but also quilting fabrics, craft paints, wooden bird houses to finish plus other arts and crafts supplies.

"Be with you in a moment," called owner Marilyn Jacobs as the bells over the door to Crafty Like a Fox jingled. "Oh, Ellie! How wonderful to see you. We were just talking about you. Were your ears ringing?"

Marilyn held instructional classes in quilting in the shop's back room, where stitching tips alternated with gossip and speculation about the "other world." Ellie wasn't entirely pleased to hear she had been the subject, and wondered whether she fell into the gossip or the weird happenings category. Or, merciful heavens, both.

"Nope, just these bells," Ellie responded, which drew a laugh. "I'm looking for yarn to make hats and mittens for the church's Cabin Fever fund raiser next month."

"Good timing," Marilyn said. "I have yarns left over from the holidays on a sale table back in that corner. And the new spring colors are up front here."

Ellie browsed through both selections, grateful that Marilyn had returned to her quilting class while she shopped. Not that Marilyn wasn't a good person, understand, but Ellie often found her tedious when it came to talking about spirits, ghosts and which buildings in Creekwood were haunted. Still, Ellie had to admit that Marilyn knew more about that sort of thing than anyone else in town, if indeed there was anything concrete to know.

Arms filled with colorful yarns, Ellie finally decided enough was enough. She carried the yarn to the checkout counter and called out to Marilyn, who bustled out from the back room. As she efficiently totaled Ellie's purchases, she launched into a wild tale about rumors that Creekwood's assisted living facility was indeed haunted.

"I did a craft class there last week and, would you believe? Half the seniors living in Maywood House are convinced that the ghost of old Oscar Maywood visits them at night."

Against her better judgment, Ellie said, "That must have them frightened. Oscar wasn't the best company when he was alive."

"Au contrare, they seem to love his company," Marilyn replied. "And even stranger, Oscar is said to be always at the bedside when one of the residents passes."

Curious in spite of herself, Ellie asked, "How do they know?" and then mentally kicked herself for encouraging Marilyn.

"You won't believe this, but the seniors said that the cat told them," Marilyn announced with a self-satisfied smile.

You're right, I don't believe it, Ellie thought. Out loud, she said, "The cat? I didn't know they had a cat at Maywood."

"Yes, it's this darling little furry Siamese with sky blue eyes," Marilyn gushed. "One old Irish fellow there swears the cat yowls like a banshee at the exact moment a resident dies. Which is weird because they named the cat Angel."

By then, Marilyn had the yarn rung up and bagged. Ellie left Crafty Like a Fox with a sigh of relief. Driving home through the early winter twilight, Ellie reviewed the day with more than one shake of her head.

After a dinner of warmed-over bean soup and cornbread, Ellie called Janelle and asked if she had any unusual mitten patterns she could borrow. Janelle wasted no time asking how Ellie's first full day at the Courier had gone. It wasn't long before the discussion turned to Marilyn and the ghost of Maywood House.

"You know, Ellie, I've heard that rumor as well," Janelle said. "One of Maywood's residents was having lunch with her old cronies at the Pinecone a few weeks ago. I overheard them talking about Oscar's visits."

"I find it hard to credit that Oscar Maywood, who was reputed to be the community curmudgeon for decades, would suddenly morph into Dr. Welby," Ellie joked.

"Well, they were saying that he comes into the rooms of those who are sensitive to spirits, then sits by their bedsides through the night, holding their hands and talking with them," Janelle added.

"Must be God's punishment for being such a grouch when he was alive, sort of like Jacob Marley in 'A Christmas Carol,'" Ellie remarked. "He died, what? 20 years or more ago, but I remember him very well. He used to come into the elementary school office to complain about the kids taking shortcuts across his lawn."

Janelle chuckled. "What do you think, Ellie? Would ghosthood mellow out a fellow like Oscar?"

"I've always liked to believe anything is possible, but after a day like today, I'm convinced it is," Ellie replied.

"Amen to that," Janelle answered.

# CHAPTER 4

When Ellie arrived at the Courier for the Tuesday afternoon editorial meeting, she found Martha disinclined to chat and the atmosphere tense. The door to Ed's office was shut tight, but she sensed someone was inside. In the rear of the office area, the editorial staff plus Gayle Warren, the sales person, were seated in tight bunches waiting in anxious silence.

Monday morning's wrap up of the PSAs and copy editing had turned out to be a little hectic but no problem to handle. But Ellie knew without having worked a Monday before that things were very different for the rest of the reporters. Ed was nowhere in sight with a paper ready to put to bed. Ellie had just assumed he would be there later to wrap up the week's edition. Now as she slid into a seat beside Kirsten, Ellie worried that her new job was going to be very short-lived.

"Okay, okay, let's get this show on the road," a fidgety Kirsten muttered. "Pardon my pun, but we all need news we can use."

Right on cue, the door to Ed's office swung open.

"Oh, my goodness, do you know who that is?" Kirsten breathed. Without waiting for Ellie to reply, she continued, "That's Ed's brother, Noel. He's the regional editor for a major Detroit newspaper. This doesn't look good."

Noel Hathaway stopped by Martha's desk and told her to hold all calls and take messages. Then he rounded the divider and strode through the editorial department, a clipboard and stack of papers gripped in one hand. He stopped abruptly in the center of the seated group and gazed around at the faces looking up at him expectantly. Noel set the papers and clipboard down on a desk and perched on its corner, one leg swinging nonchalantly.

"Okay, let's start with the bad news," Noel said. "Some of you recognize me, I'm sure. My name is Noel Hathaway, and I am Ed's younger brother. I'm here because Edith's biopsy was malignant and she is scheduled to undergo a radical mastectomy Friday at UW-Madison Hospital."

Short and brutally to the point, Ellie thought as murmurs swirled around her.

"Naturally, Ed wants to be there for her. That's why I'm here," Noel continued. "However, we have talked about Ed possibly retiring before this. Ed feels the time has come to turn active control of the Creekwood Courier over to me. Ed will continue as publisher. From this point on, I will be managing editor."

Noel's announcement was met with stunned silence.

"Now, I need to know exactly where we stand on next week's issue," Noel added. "I've looked over tomorrow's issue and it's okay as issues go. However, from now on, we are going to step up our commitment to fully, honestly representing the Creekwood community. Along with the news and coverage of city council and school board meetings, I want to see more in-depth articles on events, human interest, education and business."

Noel picked up the pile of papers at his side and thumbed through them.

"Jason, your sports reporting on the basketball games and wrestling matches are great as far as they go but I want you to go farther," Noel commented. "Talk to the athletes and the fans more, not just the coaches. Dig deeper into the emotional aspect of the game. Actual game or match coverage is more of a sidebar because almost everyone who cares was there. The real story is how they won, why they lost, what were they thinking. Got it"

Jason Whittier looked like a deer caught in a truck's headlights. "Yeah, I think I can do that."

"Don't think, dig. Oh, and your photographic skills are superb, Jason. I am especially impressed with your action shots. From here on, you're our official photographer. I need you to be available for events, hard news features and emergencies. It will free up the reporters to focus on writing. Any problem with that?"

"Ahh, no, I don't think so," Jason stammered, but now Ellie thought he looked more as if he had been struck by the truck.

"Good. We'll discuss increased hours and pay later this week. Now the hard news," Noel said, swinging without hesitation to face Kirsten. "You do an excellent job. I hope you're not planning on leaving any time soon."

"Thank you and no."

"But what I want you to do now is dig deeper," Noel said without pause. "With a weekly newspaper, we don't have the pressure of immediacy; we have the pleasure of retrospect. Write up that meeting in your usual manner, Kirsten, but take it one step further. Call community leaders, parents, whomever with the decisions and get their take on what's happening. Don't be afraid of controversy. It's out there. You know it. I know it. The whole community knows it. The Courier had better know it, too."

"And Ellie," Noel said, turning to her. "Ed told me you just started with the PSAs and meeting schedules but he also said you know the community and are detail-oriented. He believes you have the capability to become a features and education writer. I'm going to take his word for it. We're going to get you started right away."

As Noel sorted through the stack of what Ellie recognized as her PSAs, she sent a panicked look Kirsten's way. Kirsten shook her head and held up a finger. Noel looked up at that moment and caught the interaction. The side of his mouth quirked upward.

"I want you to go through these with Kirsten and decide which two events you will cover for next week's features," Noel instructed. "I expect you to write an advance article in addition to the PSA on one event and actual coverage of an event every week. Again, dig. Talk to people, get their opinions, their reactions, their recollections, their feelings. Make it come to life. Give it deeper meaning. Contact the school district and request leads on what's happening within the schools. Kirsten will continue to cover school board meetings for now. If anyone has questions, I'll be in my office until 6 or so."

No one moved a muscle until Noel had strode back out of the editorial department and closed the door to his office. Then there was a collective sigh. Ellie wasn't sure if it was in relief or fear.

"Ellie, grab those PSAs. Let's go over to the Pinecone for some tea and strategic planning," Kirsten said.

Seated across from each other in the Pinecone Café with steaming cups of tea and generous slices of courage-building cherry pie topped with double scoops of vanilla ice cream, Ellie and Kirsten sorted through the PSAs, then sorted some more.

"Okay, it looks like you could write an advance on the pie and rag rug sale at the Methodist church, with a slant on reminding people to donate sale items," Kirsten started.

Ellie interrupted her with, "What exactly is an advance?"

Kirsten leaned back in her seat and gazed steadily at Ellie. "Right. I keep forgetting you're a rookie. An advance is a story about an event coming up. Rather than just announce who, what, when and where as in the PSAs, the article should stretch beyond the obvious. In this case, what I would do is talk to the chairperson first. Find out what the committee hopes to have donated and what their fund-raising goal is, plus how the money will be used. If the event has co-chairs, try to talk to both but ask different questions so they each have equal but individual input."

Ellie thought a moment, then asked, "Should I mention that the event chair broke her ankle but is still trying to get the job done?"

Kirsten grinned. "Absolutely. That should really bring home not only the human side of the story but also how much work these events truly are."

Kirsten shuffled through the stack again. "Ah, good one. The Victorian tea and bake sale at Maywood House this Saturday afternoon. Not only does it offer great nostalgic atmosphere and the potential for excellent photos, but also you'll have a lot of people to interview. Oh, and Ellie? Be very careful to quote exactly what people say. Write it down and transcribe it as soon as possible so you don't forget what you wrote. And never, never, never throw your notes away after the story is written."

"Alibi file?"

"Absolutely!"

Both women laughed companionably, and Ellie realized how much she was starting to like Kirsten. *She has such an honest, straight forward way about her that I* admire, Ellie thought as they spooned up sinfully rich cherry pie and melting ice cream.

"On the other hand," Kirsten sighed around a mouthful. "This is just too good for words."

Ellie took a long, careful look around the Pinecone Café. From their booth at the rear of the restaurant, Ellie could see just about every single booth and table plus the long counter with its stools. Only a few people were sitting around sipping coffee at that time of day and none of them were close. Still, she leaned over the table to whisper to Kirsten because, as any small-town resident knows, even the booths have ears.

"Speaking of being good with words, I'm impressed with how Noel handled the meeting," Ellie said. "Most people would give a speech about restructuring. Noel simply restructured without giving anyone time to worry about it."

Kirsten whispered back, "Poor Jason. Did you see the look on his face? Priceless. But, you know Noel put his finger smack dab on the truth. Jason is a better-than-average photographer. Once he gets over the shock, I think he's going to really grow into the position, especially when he gets to chase fire trucks and ambulances."

"But what about me? I have no experience and not a clue," Ellie sighed.

Kirsten shook her head. "Don't sell yourself short. Ellie, you know these people, really know them. All you have to do is talk to them and take notes, then tell their stories. Find something unique, unusual about this event and ask for everyone's opinion. Be sure to book Jason to take photos. Before you come in Monday morning, email your story and we'll go over the two stories. Then I'll copy-edit your stories so we have a double-check system."

As Ellie finished the last bite of pie, she unexpectedly understood why this would be harder than Kirsten knew. For more than 30 years, Ellie had been an integrated part of the Creekwood Community. Becoming an observer and reporter would now set her apart from the crowd. She wouldn't blend in as usual, and that made her wonder if her friends and neighbors would change their attitudes toward her. Would they still talk freely? Avoid her? Tell the truth?

Driving home, Ellie decided that the best way to handle Saturday's assignment might be to not arrive alone. She took a detour to Janelle's house and arranged for the two of them to go to Maywood House together.

Writing the advance on the Methodist Church's pie and rag rug sale turned out to be a, well, piece of pie for Ellie. Both chairpersons had been enthusiastic, forthcoming and delighted that it was Ellie who would be publishing the extra coverage. The selling point had been her interview with Maggie Lawrence, who at the age of 87, still hand-made rag rugs for the sale. Jason had taken two photos, one of Maggie at work on a rug and one with the chairpersons putting price tags on finished rugs, featuring Melody with her leg propped on a stool. Kirsten has pronounced it very satisfactory. Noel accepted the story with no comment, from which Ellie inferred she had done all right.

As Ellie and Janelle stepped inside Maywood House, Ellie took a deep breath. It was crowded early, which was a good sign that the event would prove successful. She had hoped to work on her story inconspicuously but Maywood House's administrator spotted her immediately.

"Mrs. Franklin, we are just thrilled that you will be writing up our Victorian Tea," Thomas Wagner gushed. Taking her hand and tucking it under his arm, he continued, "I want you to meet our oldest resident, Ms. Maybelle Swain, who has lived here since Maywood House opened its doors."

As Wagner propelled Ellie across the entryway and into the parlor, she shot a startled glance back at a widely grinning Janelle. Stepping into the parlor, though, Ellie forgot her discomfort and gazed about in amazement. The elegantly proportioned room was papered in a velvet plush pale plum with deep plum accents and dainty cream stripes. The stately furniture, upholstered in purple and forest green, reflected the charm and serenity of a bygone era. Delicate watercolors of wood violets in antique frames lined the walls.

Maybelle Swain held court as one of the tea's official hostesses, shaking hands and nodding regally as guests filtered through Maywood House's rooms on their way back to the dining area. Tiny, wearing a soft silvery dress with sensible black shoes, Maybelle had bright blue eyes that twinkled beneath a halo of feathery white hair. She beckoned to Ellie to sit beside her.

Turning to Ellie after greeting another guest, Maybelle said, "I am delighted to meet you, Mrs. Franklin. I have heard your name mentioned many times thought the years."

"Good things, I hope," Ellie murmured, flipping open her notepad and preparing to write down what Maybelle shared.

"Oh, very good indeed," Maybelle remarked. "And now I hear that you are starting a new career in reporting? How exciting! I just wish Oscar were here so he could be included in the interviews. He would so enjoy all the hustle and bustle in his home."

"Oscar? You mean Oscar Maywood, the former owner? I was under the impression that Oscar Maywood was reclusive to a fault, though I did see him a few times in the school superintendent's office," Ellie replied. "But Mr. Maywood died many years ago."

"Why yes, of course he did," Maybelle continued.

"You mean he's here in spirit?"

"Oh, very much so," Maybelle chuckled. "Just last night, he told me that, if he had known how nice it felt to have people around who understood him, he would have opened his home to old folks while he was still alive."

"You say you talked to him last night?" Ellie ventured, quickly revising her opinion of Maybelle's mental state.

"Oh, certainly. We chat nearly every night," Maybelle said. "Oscar visits almost every single one of us during the night. We old people don't sleep so well, you see. So Oscar keeps us company, listening to our complaints and telling stories about Creekwood when it was first settled."

"Almost everyone?" Ellie prompted.

"Some just can't seem to see or hear Oscar," Maybelle confided. "It's not that they don't believe. I feel it's because they simply aren't sensitive enough."

Ellie made notes on her pad as Maybelle looked on with approval.

"Who sees Oscar?"

"My dear, it's easier to tell you who doesn't. Andy Maxwell and George Simpson don't. They are residents. And the head of housekeeping, Judith Anderson, doesn't seem to see him even when we know he's standing right there in plain sight!"

"Does Mr. Wagner see Oscar?"

"My goodness, no, not that one." Maybelle said, thus consigning Thomas Wagner to the ranks of the insensitive.

Just then, Jason arrived with his camera case. Ellie arranged for him to take photos of Maybelle, then more in the dining room where English tea was being served. Leaving him to his work, Ellie wandered through the crowded dining room where tempting trays of finger sandwiches, cookies and scones were attracting a lot of attention. Glancing around, she quickly stepped into the kitchen where Judith Anderson was loading trays and directing traffic. The first question was easy.

"Wow! How in the world did you put this all together?" Ellie asked Judith in a moment of relative calm.

Judith studied Ellie, making special note of the note pad. Ellie knew Judith to be a person who didn't suffer fools. She could be cooperative or not, depending on the time and circumstance. Ellie held her breath and waited.

"Working, huh?"

"Yeah, first one," Ellie replied.

Judith seemed to relax. "This is our first Victorian Tea at Maywood House," Judith began formally. "We started working on the plans almost one year ago."

"Why, I mean, how did you come up with the concept of an English tea?"

Judith shook her head ruefully. "You won't believe this but the residents insisted we host some kind of party that would be open to the public. Usually, we plan parties for the residents and their immediate families, but they said Maywood House was meant to be a gathering place for everyone and to be an integral part of the community. So, here we are."

Ellie thought frantically for a way to introduce the subject of Oscar. But, before she could ask other leading questions, Judith continued.

"I guess you could say they think they had a little prompting," Judith said with a glance over her shoulder at the doorway to the dining room. "They told us it was Oscar Maywood's idea. Now how ridiculous is that?"

Ellie had to agree with Judith in spirit. Having met the cantankerous old recluse more than once, she just couldn't see it, either. But then, Judith surprised her with a curious admission.

"You know, I just cannot bring myself to believe in ghosts," Judith confessed. "But every now and then, when I'm alone in the pantry late at night, I could swear that someone else is there. You know the feeling, Ellie? I just know someone is standing behind me, looking over my shoulder. But when I turn around, there's no one. It fairly makes the hair stand up on the back of my neck. Don't quote me on that, please."

Ellie spent most of Sunday afternoon on her laptop, working on a draft of the Maywood House Victorian Tea. Along with describing the atmosphere, the refreshments and other details, she wove in comments from Maybelle, Judith and several others about the ghost of Oscar Maywood. With considerable trepidation, she sent them to Kirsten early Monday morning.

"Don't laugh," she warned Kirsten.

"I promise," Kirsten replied before pulling the stories up on her computer. Still, within a few minutes, Ellie heard Kirsten's muffled giggles.

"You promised," Ellie said indignantly.

"Oh, Ellie, it's not your writing style that's funny. This story is good. In fact, it's wonderful as a human-interest feature," Kirsten said with a huge grin. "What's hilarious is that Noel wanted us to stir things up, and this will definitely do it."

"Oh, no. Oh, my God," Ellie exclaimed. "We can't publish it. We'll get all kinds of flack from everyone. I didn't think. I didn't realize…"

"Whoa, Ellie," Kirsten said, making a time-out sign with her hands. "That's exactly what we want, remember? And it is what Noel wants. He said he doesn't want business as usual. And the bottom line is, lots of people already have heard the rumors about Oscar's ghost. They just don't bring it out into the light for fear of feeling like idiots. It's like that old saw about ignoring the elephant in the room. You simply can't. It's there."

Ellie slumped in her chair with a sigh of chagrin. "So now what do we do?"

"We give it the bomb test," Kirsten said, turning back to her monitor. "We drop it on Noel and wait for the fallout."

Ellie continued keying in last-minute PSAs and proofreading weekend stories. It seemed like only seconds before the door to the editor's office flew open and Noel charged into the editorial area.

"Victorian Tea is a spirited affair? Did you make this up, Ellie?" he roared without so much as a "good morning."

"No, I did not," Ellie stated indignantly. "Do you want to see my notes?"

Noel glared down at Ellie, then looked over at Kirsten who was grinning like a Cheshire cat.

"Actually, I've heard the rumors that Maywood House is haunted, too," Kirsten said.

"Then why didn't you write about it?" Noel demanded.

"Because it is not hard news," Kirsten countered. "And we didn't have a features…"

"Writer. I know," Noel interrupted. "Ellie, do you stand behind this information? Is it exactly what they said? Word for word?"

"Yes, I do and yes, it is," Ellie said emphatically.

Noel tipped his head, letting his glasses slip down to the end of his nose as he stared down at her. He shook his head once, then replied, "Then it goes. front page, top of the fold as a matter of fact."

# CHAPTER 5

The sun was barely peeking over the trees when Ellie gave up on sleep. She had spent a fitful night second-guessing herself over and over again on the Maywood House ghost story. Getting up, she padded down to the kitchen in her nightgown and slippers to put on a pot of strong coffee. Ellie lit candles on the counter and kitchen table, and then made a list of the things she wanted to accomplish.

Feeling antsy, and not content with that, she pulled her private collection of recipes from its drawer and gathered the ingredients for chocolate chip cookies. Between the familiar routine of baking and the bracing aroma of French roast coffee, Ellie started feeling a bit more settled. By the time she had poured her first cup and shoved a baking sheet of cookies in the oven, she felt more ready to face the day.

Dressed in navy slacks and her favorite sweater, a silky soft turtleneck in shades of blue that started at the neck ice pale and blended skillfully to deepest cobalt at the ribbed waist, Ellie packed a generous number of warm cookies in an attractive plastic container. Then she drove downtown to the Courier office. Ellie put the cookies on the table in the lunchroom and sat down at her desk just as Jennifer came through distributing copies of the Courier from a tall stack on a dolly.

"Hot off the press," Jennifer said, plopping a newspaper on Ellie's desk. "Boy, I truly do love your ghost story! That ought to stir things up around here."

Ellie groaned. "Unfortunately, I think you're right."

"Oh, don't worry about the locals," Jennifer sniffed. "A few will complain, a few more will praise the story to the skies and the majority will sit in their recliners savoring the controversy. They'll pretend it's all hooey but deep down inside, they'll be titillated."

"Titillated? Oh, gee," Ellie moaned. "That paints an awful picture."

Kirsten breezed in, plunked her briefcase down on her desk, and glanced down at the Courier. "Wow, great photo! Jason's already living up to his potential." Taking a deep breath, then another, Kirsten added, "Do I smell chocolate chip cookies?"

Ellie pointed her in the general direction of the lunchroom, picked up the paper, and unfolded it. Under a 48-point headline that read, "Victorian Tea is a spirited affair," Jason's photo took up the center with her story split on both sides and beneath. In it, Maybelle Swain perched on the upholstered chair in Maywood House's parlor, accepting a cup of tea from a tray offered by a staff member. Curled under her left arm was a fluffy Siamese cat that appeared to be gazing at something past the other side of Maybelle's head.

"That must be Angel, the house pet. I didn't see her Saturday," Ellie mused. "She looks more Himalayan than Siamese. I wonder what she's looking at."

"Who knows. Cats are weird. And you know what's even stranger?" Kirsten said around a mouth full of cookie. She pointed to the headline. "Noel didn't change the heading. In fact, I believe he didn't change a single word. Now that's amazing for a big-time editor."

"What big-time editor?"

All three women jumped and turned to find Noel standing right behind them. *Now I really know what Judith was referring to when she told me about things creeping up behind her*, Ellie thought distractedly.

"Ellie, can I see you in my office?" Noel didn't wait for an answer but turned and headed back toward the front of the newspaper office.

Ellie shot an alarmed look at Kirsten and Jennifer before picking up her notepad.

"Hmmmmm," said Kirsten.

"Hmmmmm," said Jennifer. "Why are you taking your notepad?"

"Alibi file," both Ellie and Kirsten said at once, then burst out laughing.

Ellie's smile faded as she trailed after Noel. Entering Ed's former office, she found Noel already seated behind the desk, leaning back with his hands tucked behind his

74

head just as his brother Ed was wont to do. Ellie slid into a chair and took a deep breath, then started when Noel abruptly sat up and leaned forward.

"Do you believe there's a ghost in Maywood House?" he asked without preamble.

"No, not really," Ellie replied hesitantly. "But I believe the residents think there is."

"Excellent! Exactly the way you broached the subject," Noel beamed. "Ed was right. You have good instincts, Ellie. The story is intriguing without being presumptuous, and sensitive to the residents' feelings without implying any skepticism. Straightforward, honest, simple. Now, how much did Kirsten help you?"

"She made a number of suggestions that I followed," Ellie said thoughtfully. "And she helped me re-organize the information so it read smoother."

"But the content was solely yours?" At Ellie's nod, he continued, "And you learned from her help?"

"I certainly did," Ellie said. "In several places, I knew what I wanted to say but the words didn't seem to flow. Kirsten taught me to read it over and over in my mind until I thought them through in a natural manner. Instead of being stilted, the words fell into place more like conversation than writing an essay."

"Good, because I want you to write more than a couple of stories each week," Noel announced to her shock. Rifling through a pile of paper on his desk, he picked out one and said, "Take this insipid news release on the proposed statewide legalization on marijuana, and personalize it to Creekwood."

At Ellie's look of dismay, Noel explained, "I don't ever want to see canned PR stories without a local hook in the Courier from this point on. Talk to people, Ellie. They know you. Ask anyone that you feel will be directly impacted by the law's enactment. Get a strong point of view from the school district, the police department, the mayor, shop owners, the clinic, churches, and residents. I know you know people in Creekwood who would be extremely upset if marijuana was legalized. Ask them how they feel about Chicago's law making smoking and carrying marijuana a ticketing issue instead of making arrests. Go for it, girl!"

Ellie picked up the news release and made a dash for the office door before Noel had any more great ideas. Just as she was about to make a safe escape, she heard Noel clear his throat and say, "Hey, Ellie?"

She paused at the wistful tone of his voice and looked back. That was when she first noticed he had lovely eyes, deep coffee brown with thick lashes beneath his glasses.

"Did I smell chocolate chip cookies out in the editorial room?"

Ellie almost laughed at the relief she felt. "Yes, you did," she replied. "I cook when I get nervous."

"And you're nervous about how this ghost story is going to be received? Well, if baking is how you react to pressure, we'll just have to keep you on edge most of the time."

Ellie fled past an open-mouthed Martha, who was waving a fistful of messages at her, and back to the questionable safety of her desk. Behind her, she heard Noel chuckling softly on his way to the lounge.

The clock had barely reached 9 a.m. when Ellie fielded her first call on the ghost story.

"I love it!" Janelle crowed. "And the photo is priceless. That cat seems to be looking at a ghost no one else can see."

Ellie glanced down at her desk copy and gulped. It did indeed look as if Angel saw something near a bookcase that no one else did, or could. No wonder Noel had left the headline alone, Ellie thought. It's just almost too perfect. Oh, my, am I going to get calls.

After Ellie ended Janelle's call, Kirsten leaned toward her and said, "A word of advice? Agree with anyone who loves it and do not disagree with anyone who doesn't. Listen politely and then suggest they write a letter to the editor with their concerns. And remind them that you don't make the news; you simply report it as you see it. Be firm."

"And polite," Ellie repeated. "But won't we get a bunch of angry letters?"

"I certainly hope so," Kirsten grinned. "Letters to the editor are sort of legitimate gossip as long as they don't degenerate into vendettas. They are among the biggest reasons why weekly newspapers sell, along with the obits, of course, and especially small-town ones like the Courier. Those letters validate our reporting. Readers relish controversy. Besides, you didn't write about anything that almost everyone in town hasn't already heard. Truth is, we haven't had something this deliciously weird to stir things up in too long a time."

Kirsten brushed crumbs from her fingers and murmured, "Speaking of delicious…"

Frowning, Ellie watched her head back to the lounge as her phone rang. Ellie barely got the words "Editorial, Ellie Franklyn speaking" out before Marilyn of Crafty Like a Fox" fame gushed, "Ellie, you wonderful person, you. I've been waiting all my life for someone official to admit there's more to this life than what we can see or feel. I'm so glad you're on our side."

"Ummmmm," Ellie got out. Official? On our side? Oh, yippee!

Fortunately, Marilyn was so wrapped up in what she felt was a validation of her belief in spirits that Ellie couldn't get a word in edgewise to protest. Kirsten's advice about not arguing with a reader's opinion was not even necessary as Marilyn rhapsodized about the ghost story. Things went a bit differently when Maywood House administrator Tom Wagner called.

"Now, Ellie, I know you wrote this story to entertain," Tom stated. "And I really do like how you covered the tea. In fact, that part is excellent. But I feel I need to comment on the ghost of Oscar."

"I fully understand," Ellie responded. "And I'm happy that you liked the story overall. May I suggest you write a letter to the editor, Noel Hathaway, expressing your concerns? That way, everyone will be able to appreciate your position."

"That's a wonderful idea," Tom replied. "I was going to submit a note thanking everyone who came anyway, so adding a remark or two on the supposed ghost makes good sense. Thanks for the suggestion. And Ellie, keep up the good work."

By lunchtime, Ellie was ready to admit things hadn't gone as badly as she had imagined. Still, she knew those who hadn't called her directly were busy whispering behind her back. The Creekwood grapevine was nothing if not healthy and thriving. She sighed, "I just hope most people don't think I'm a crackpot," and with a little shudder, she added, "like Marilyn."

After lunch, Ellie settled in to line up interviews for the marijuana article. She was just finishing her list when Jason bounded into the editorial area, bringing a blast of cold air and excitement in his wake.

"Kirsten! There's a big fire!"

Kirsten looked away from her monitor as Jason fell into one of the chairs in front of Ellie's desk.

"Where?"

"It's those old twin barns out on Madison Road," he shouted.

Kirsten shook her head. "Calm down, Jason. That's probably good for a photo with an extended cutline about the loss of a community landmark…"

"But, Kirsten, they both caught on fire at the same time," Jason interrupted her.

"Oh, that's different," Kirsten said as she stood and reached for her coat.

Slinging her purse and reporter kit over one shoulder at the same time, she glanced across at Ellie.

"You have all week to work on that story. Want to come along?"

Ellie didn't have to think twice. She grabbed her coat and purse, then followed Jason and Kirsten out. On the way, Kirsten paused at Martha's desk.

"Martha, we have a probable arson at the twin barns on Madison Road," she reported. "I'll call in as soon as I know more."

As they piled into their cars, Jason in his and Ellie with Kirsten, Kirsten said, "It's a good policy to always let someone in the office know where you are going and why. It's not only a safety factor, but it keeps everyone in the loop. This way, if Noel feels he needs more information quickly or decides to come out there personally, we haven't left him wondering or asking where we are."

Ellie nodded. That made good sense.

As they wound along narrow country roads through corn stubble fields and woods, Ellie could see double towering columns of ugly black smoke underlit with red ahead. Even if Kirsten didn't know how to get to the location, the smoke bannered across the winter blue sky pinpointed the site.

"How far is the fire from town?" Kirsten asked.

"Between seven and eight miles," Ellie replied.

"We can already see the smoke. The barns are probably going to be a total loss. What can you tell me about them?"

"Well, I believe they were built in the early 1920s, part of a big dairy farm operated by the Davis family," Ellie said. "We'll need to check for sure but the historical society will know. They may even have old photos. The farm has been deserted for years, possibly decades."

Kirsten was silent for a moment. "Good, then could you do the background and historical side of the story while I cover the actual fire and investigation?" At Ellie's nod, she continued, "Great! I'm sure many long-time residents will have memories to share about the barns and the family that lived there. We'll work it as a team."

Kirsten pulled her car smartly in beside Jason's and the three walked through a welter of police and fire vehicles. The still air was dense with smoke, the smell of burning old timber choking, the crackle of fire ominous. Firefighters clustered in groups, aiming thick arcs of water at the fire. But Ellie could see that it was already too late to save even a part of both barns. As she cautiously approached, one of the roofs collapsed with a roar, sending a billowing cloud of spark-filled smoke high into the sky.

"Jason, get back!

Kirsten thrust her notepad and pen at Ellie and dashed forward to where Jason stood transfixed by the fire. He was so involved in taking shot after shot that he didn't realize how far he had ventured into the fire zone. Before Kirsten could reach him, one of the firefighters grabbed Jason's coat sleeve and pulled him roughly back toward the small group of onlookers with a stern word and a pointed finger.

"For crying out loud, Jason, use the zoom," Kirsten chided as he sheepishly joined them. "We don't want to lose you so early in your new career."

Ellie turned away from them to gaze back at the fire. She marveled at the way the hungry flames licked the old wood like a ravenous wild animal, devouring the old barns and swallowing time. She was confused and somewhat frightened at what she was feeling as she looked into the fire, a mixture of fascination, exhilaration, and fear. She shook her head and resolutely turned away. In the growing crowd behind the fire lines, she saw Mack Davis, one of the few family members remaining in the area whose grandparents had worked the farm. As she started toward him to begin interviews for her side article, she also saw Noel standing next to the fire chief.

Noel glanced toward the fire and saw her. His eyes widened and he excused himself to the chief. Striding across the rough trampled ground, he stopped abruptly in front of her, blocking her way.

"What are you doing here?" he demanded.

"I'm helping Kirsten by doing a sidebar feature," Ellie snapped back. "The grandson of the family who built these barns is here and I want to interview him before he leaves. Now, if you would please excuse me."

Ellie stepped around Noel and headed toward the spot where Mack was still standing. She could feel Noel's stare burning into her back the whole way. As she stood talking to Mack, she could see Noel talking to Kirsten and Jason out of the corner of her eye. The exchange didn't look friendly.

Mack was saying, "… such good memories of growing up and spending summers here with my grandparents. We lived in Milwaukee, and my parents believed it would be good for me and my brothers to get out of the city for the summer. Those barns weren't just for housing cows and storing hay. We played hide and seek in the loft. We had barn dances and Halloween parties, harvest celebrations, all sorts of wonderful times. Why, I kissed my first girlfriend in that stone milk shed. And now..." he gazed sorrowfully at the burning barns, eyes wet with unshed tears. "Now they are gone. To tell you the truth, I always envisioned them as gracefully crumbling into the earth over a long time, not going up in flames. It's just not the way I wanted them to end."

He turned to point to the old limestone farmhouse with its caved-in porch that wrapped around three sides of the structure.

"We had some good times in there, too," he added. "Birthday parties, toffee pulling parties, and oh, Thanksgiving and Christmas on the farm. God, how I loved it all. How I wish I could have shared it with my children, but my grandparents moved off the farm before I married. My parents were in no position to give up their jobs and work a dairy farm. I come out here every once in a while to walk around the property and remember. And now, the barns are gone."

Ellie could hear the heartache in every word. Whatever would possess someone to burn down the barns, she wondered. Why would anyone do such a thing? It made no sense to her, and for that reason, she felt a frission of disquiet.

"Ellie, ready to go back?" Kirsten called.

Ellie said goodbye to Mack and joined Kirsten at her car. Looking back at the two blackened, smoking rectangles where ancient metal stations still marked the milking room, she asked, "Was it arson?"

"Yup, you don't have two fires starting in two different buildings at the same time by accident," Kirsten confirmed. "Such a shame even though they were no longer being used. I can't believe the stupidity of someone, doing something like this."

Ellie murmured agreement but that niggling little idea that the senseless fire was not a matter of stupidity but something much more ominous kept poking into her thoughts.

Back in the office, Ellie rough drafted the interview and her impressions, then started a list of people to supplement the story. Before she could make a single phone call, the president of the historical society was put through to her.

"Oh, Ellie, isn't it awful? A whole chunk of our history lost," Georgia Buckingham cried. "Those beautiful old barns were nearly 100 years old. I still can't believe they're gone."

And without prompting, Georgia began a rambling but fairly comprehensive history of the twin barns from the barn-raising party that drew dozens of neighbors and down through the years. Ellie asked if there were old photographs available and was delighted when Georgia replied that the society had a folder filled with black-and-white pictures including one at the original barn raising.

"Ellie, is it true? Was it arson? I mean, that's what I'm hearing but you know the grapevine around here. It often grows some pretty strange branches," Georgia said.

Ellie decided to err on the side of caution. "It's still being investigated, Georgia, so we don't have confirmation on that. The fire chief did describe it as suspicious."

To Ellie's relief, Georgia seems to accept her answer. Kirsten nodded her approval as well, which gave Ellie a warm feeling. Instincts and a strong sense of discretion honed through years of dealing with irate parents and frustrated teachers were paying off once again, she mused. The fire story practically wrote itself. Ellie avoided referring to the investigation and focused on memories and feelings. It was easy because she identified strongly with how people felt about losing a treasured part of their community history. It was her community, too. But, later that night, as she lay awake in bed with details of the day popping up, two things really bothered her.

One was the way Noel Hathaway challenged her right to be at the fire scene. I mean, who does he think he is, besides the editor, she fumed. He specifically asked me to step up the Courier's coverage and to help make events more meaningful to readers. Does he think I can do this from behind a desk? I don't understand him at all. What is his problem?

But, the second thought was far more troubling. The barns were about seven miles from Creekwood, in the center of a quiet and relatively unpopulated area of the countryside. Someone who knew the area had to have set the fires. Itinerate passers-through would never find them except by accident. And this was obviously no accident.

So it has to be a resident of the immediate area, Ellie concluded.

Next, it was highly unlikely that teens were involved unless one or more of them skipped school. Then they would have had to have access to a vehicle. And with the traffic on that country road light, anyone living along it would take note of a strange car passing through. The attendance office would know who had been absent that afternoon, but Ellie knew that Kirsten would not be given that information. Student information was strictly confidential when she had worked in the office, and with the reinforced rules on privacy in effect, the only people who would be able to check on absentees were the police and fire investigators. Besides, it hadn't felt like a kid thing.

No, Ellie decided, it felt more like an adult had deliberately driven out into the peaceful woods, probably from a different direction. He _ or she, although Ellie shrunk from believing a woman would do such a thing _ may have parked his vehicle along another roadway and hiked through the woods to the barns. Once there, he had set a fire in both barns and, once he was sure the fires would take, had quickly retreated to where he had parked the vehicle and then fled. No one would see the vehicle and possibly recognize it. No one would see the arsonist as he moved silently through the woods.

That felt right, but Ellie knew it was just a theory. There was really no way to know exactly what had occurred because there didn't seem to have been any witnesses. What remained was one burning question: Why?

# CHAPTER 6

Ellie sighed deeply and stared out the kitchen window into the darkness. She couldn't remember anyone warning her that, after the funeral and burial, she would have to face a long, painful series of firsts. Someone probably did. She knew too many widows in town who understood firsthand what losing a husband was like. Today was shaping up to be another sad day.

First, it had been her birthday late in January. Jerry had never been extravagant with gifts, but he had been thoughtful, even romantic. For her birthday, he had always placed a card for her on the breakfast table with their coffees. And Jerry had taken her to dinner, wherever and whatever she wanted. Often Janelle and Don had joined them, the four spending happy hours together over excellent food.

This year, Janelle and Don had invited Ellie over to their home for dinner, a sharp break from tradition. Ellie had welcomed the change. She just couldn't face sitting in her favorite restaurant without Jerry there, where the likelihood of a tearful breakdown was better than average. Kirsten, Martha, and Jennifer had treated her to lunch at the PC, where broccoli cheese soup, cranberry scones and an enormous piece of lemon meringue pie helped fill some of the emptiness.

Jerry's birthday in early February had always been another cause for celebration, with Ellie presenting the card and cooking Jerry's favorite dishes. Again, Janelle and Don had often joined them around the dining table, sipping wine and laughing over the passing of time. This time, Janelle had called to see if she wanted to come over, but Ellie had opted to spend the evening alone with her memories.

Today was Valentine's Day. In the past, Ellie would come down to the kitchen to find fancy heart-shaped boxes of chocolates and little gifts. Jerry knew her pretty well. The gifts varied from red candles, floral stationery, or a notepad design she hadn't ferreted out for herself. This morning, there was nothing on the table, but there was a new, aching hole inside Ellie that felt as if it could never be filled.

"Stop this pity party immediately," Ellie told herself. "What I need is … French toast!"

Jerry had never been a pancake or French toast fan. He was more of an eggs, sausage, and American fries kind of guy, which had been fine with Ellie. But now she craved French toast, a lot of it. Well, two pieces of Texas toast, maybe. Ellie beat a couple of eggs and stirred in cinnamon, vanilla and a touch of half-and-half. She laid two pieces of bread on a plate and poured the eggs over them, turning them and letting them soak in all the liquid while she pulled out the frying pan, butter, and syrup. Just the smell of the French toast cooking lifted her spirits a little.

Ellie had just cleaned her plate and poured another cup of coffee when her cell phone rang. She glanced at the clock. 6:17 a.m. Who on earth would call at this time of the day? Ellie snapped the phone open, but before she could say "hello," an excited voice boomed in her ear.

"Ellie, are you awake?"

"If I wasn't, I am now, Noel," Ellie replied wryly. Before she could ask why he was calling so early, he continued.

"Good, because I need you here right now," Noel said, breathlessly. "Maywood House is on fire."

"Dear Lord," Ellie exclaimed. "Is everyone okay?"

"No fatalities, thank goodness, but several of the residents were transported to UW-Madison for smoke inhalation treatment and observation," Noel said. "I need you as quickly as you can get here. Kirsten is covering the hard news, but I want you to write a companion piece on how the community is reacting to this tragedy."

"How will I…" Ellie began.

"Don't worry about finding them," Noel responded. "There are about 250 people standing along the roadway. Some of them are crying. You'll have no trouble at all getting reactions."

Noel hung up and Ellie rushed upstairs to dress. She pulled flannel-lined jeans, a long-sleeved T-shirt and a heavy sweater out of drawers, then found her thermal socks. Downstairs, she filled Jerry's old thermos with the rest of the coffee, added a healthy dose of hazelnut creamer and found her down parka in the hallway closet. Outside, it was barely light but she could see a dense black cloud of smoke underlit with that telltale red rising in the direction of Maywood House. As she put the car in gear and backed out of the driveway, Ellie could feel tears welling up in her own eyes.

The police department had all of the roads around Maywood House blocked to traffic, so Ellie parked a couple of blocks away and walked up the hill toward the fire. Kirsten was standing fairly close to the fire chief and his officers, trying to overhear anything newsworthy. Noel was right, Ellie thought. Hundreds of Creekwood residents lined the sidewalks and streets, held at a safe distance by the police squads. And many of them were in tears.

"They're already calling it a fire of suspicious origin," Kirsten said by way of greeting. "The fire started at the rear of the house either next to, or on, the back porch. It had help getting started, and was raging by the time the alarm sounded. They are trying their best but it had too much of a start. I'm afraid the original part of the house is a goner."

Ellie heard a roar like the sound of a freight train and turned to face the fire. The entire rear of Maywood House was engulfed in flame. Little snakes of fire crawled along the eaves and overhang, nipping at the gingerbread trim. Ellie could see the paint blistering on the window frames and porch trim.

"What you're hearing is fire breaking through a wall and finding more air," Kirsten said as the roar increased.

Now Ellie could see flames through the home's front windows on both floors. A side window exploded outward, causing several firefighters to leap back from the wall just as flames shot out.

"Oh, my God," Ellie breathed just as the walls trembled and the gabled roof crashed downward into the house, displacing a huge billow of smoke. Flames shot skyward at least 50 feet. "That wonderful, beautiful house is going to be a total loss. How am I going to talk to people about this? Many worked here, and many more had elderly parents or other relatives who lived here as well."

"Don't worry, they'll want to talk," Kirsten encouraged. "Besides, you're one of them."

It struck Ellie that Kirsten still felt like an outsider, having only worked in Creekwood for a bit more than a year. She did have an advantage. She knew these people. She had known Oscar Maywood, too, if only through listening to his complaints in the school office about kids cutting across his lawn. Yes, she told herself, she could do this for Maywood House and Oscar. She wasn't likely to hear anything she didn't feel personally.

Ellie started with Mayor George Larson's wife, Nina, whose mother had been a Maywood House resident for many years. After more than two hours of working the crowd around the fire site, Ellie drove to the Courier office. Shivering with cold and emotion, she hung her parka on the back of her chair and began transcribing her notes into a rough draft. The coffee in her thermos was still fairly hot, but Ellie put on a fresh pot in the lunchroom, knowing the others soon would be coming in, cold and emotionally drained.

Within an hour, Ellie had a passable draft ready. When Kirsten came in, smelling of acrid smoke, she took about 10 minutes to scan through Ellie's copy.

"Wow, you really nailed it, Ellie," Kirsten said, grinning. "I just marked a few places where I felt it needed smoothing out."

"Thanks, Kirsten," Ellie replied. "What's the latest?"

"Definitely arson," Kirsten murmured, turning to her monitor. "Breaks my heart. Why would anyone do such a terrible thing? It's just pure luck the staff was able to get everyone out with minor smoke inhalation and a few non-life-threatening injuries. We're looking at a major criminal investigation. Arson and attempted murder. The state fire marshal is on his way."

Ellie glanced at the clock. "Bet you didn't eat," she said.

Kirsten groaned. "I don't bet on sure things."

"How about I bring you some hot soup and scones from the PC?"

"Oh, please."

"And I put a fresh pot of coffee on, too," Ellie said.

Without asking, Ellie brought back a mug well laced with half-and-half and sugar for Kirsten, who was still shivering.

"Mmmmm," was her only response as she crouched over the keyboard, fingers flying.

After a mercy run to the PC for Kirsten, Ellie sent her story with Kirsten's feature to Noel's editorial file, logged off on her computer and headed for home. The only thing on Ellie's mind was a hot shower, fresh clothes and a defrosted container of chicken noodle soup.

But as she pulled into the driveway and paused for the garage door to open, she thought she saw a pale flicker of movement from the corner of her eye. Ellie looked around but didn't see anything. She drove the car into the garage, lowered the garage door, and started to open the kitchen door. A sooty, bedraggled cat smelling strongly of wood smoke appeared at her feet, gazing up at her.

Ellie stared. "It can't be," she thought.

Ellie swung the door open and the little cat sauntered into the house without the least bit of hesitation. Ellie followed her into the kitchen where the cat stopped in front of the refrigerator and gazed back at Ellie, a clear hint that she was hungry. Ellie shook her head in a bewildered fashion, set her purse on the counter and started to take off her parka.

"Mrrrowwww."

Jerry and Ellie had kept a few small dogs as pets through the years, but she had never owned a cat. Still, she thought, their needs must be about the same. Ellie pulled a small plastic bowl from a cupboard and filled it with cool water. The cat began lapping the water greedily while Ellie rummaged through another cupboard and found a can of tuna. At the sound of the can opener, the cat looked up expectantly and licked her chops. When Ellie put a saucer down for the cat, she daintily picked at the chunks of tuna, purring contentedly.

Ellie watched the cat eat for a moment or two, then flipped open her cell phone and called the one person she knew could help.

"Creekwood Post Office, Helen Lipton speaking."

"Helen, this is Ellie Franklin," Ellie began, but before she could continue, Helen jumped in with a dozen questions about the fire. Finally, Ellie was able to bring up the burning subject for which she had called.

"Helen, I came home and found a cat in my garage," Ellie said. "In fact, she invited herself into the house. And what's weird is, I think it's Angel from Maywood House."

After a long pause, Helen said, "Really. That is weird. Because Tom Wagner called me to ask if anyone had seen Angel. She was among the missing. What are you going to do about her?"

"I don't know," Ellie answered. "I suppose someone else might want her, like Tom or perhaps Maybelle Swain."

"Well, until that's settled, you are going to need some stuff," Helen said. "After I close up, I'll bring over a litter box and some supplies to get you started. If someone decides he or she wants her, you can just clean them and give them back."

"Helen, that's wonderful of you," Ellie replied. "And you can probably recognize the cat, even if it isn't Angel, right?"

"Probably. So I'll be over just after 5:30 p.m."

Ellie put the teakettle on, and sat at the kitchen table gazing at the cat. The cat returned the favor. After a few moments, Ellie called Janelle to catch her up on the day's events. When she got to the part about the cat showing up at her door, Janelle was clearly flabbergasted.

"You've got to be kidding, right? No? Mercy, Ellie, that's downright spooky."

"And what's worse, she acts like she belongs here, Janelle. I called Helen Lipton who said she'd be over after she closed the post office. The cat is all sooty and smoky, but it might not be Angel. At least, she doesn't act as if she were hurt, thank goodness."

"Yeah, right," Janelle snorted. "Creekwood is loaded with feline refuges from campfires. Oh, Ellie, face it.

You've just had a Marilyn Jacobs moment. The ghost cat from Maywood House!"

"Oh, good grief, Janelle. That cat practically ate a whole can of tuna. She's no ghost," Ellie replied. "But what if Helen doesn't recognize her?"

"Call Vic the Vet," Janelle suggested. "He knows just about every animal in the county personally."

"Good idea."

And just about everyone in the county knew Victor Patterson, even though almost no one called him by his last name. He was simply Vic the Vet, and he'd been Creekwood's one and only veterinarian for longer than Jerry and Ellie had lived there. Ellie called him immediately after ending her call to Janelle.

"Angel is one of my patients. I'd have to see the cat, but I can tell you up front that I don't know of any other cats in the entire area that resemble her," Vic the Vet said. "In fact, that was the oddest thing. Angel just showed up on Maywood House's doorstep about two years ago. She's a long-haired Siamese and not that common. Plus, Siamese are not known to be outdoor cats so there was a lot of speculation at the time about who might have dumped her off."

"You mean she just showed up at the door over there like she did here?"

"Yup," Vic the Vet confirmed. "Ms. Lipton should recognize her, but if she doesn't, bring the little one in."

Faced with a long, dark winter afternoon, and an even longer, darker evening, Ellie mixed up a batch of walnut fudge brownies and put them in the oven. Angel, as Ellie was already calling her, proved to be a warmth-loving critter who curled up on the rug in front of the stove to soak up the heat. When the brownies were cooled and frosted, Ellie lit a fire in the living room fireplace and settled on the couch with a new mystery from Cross-Eyed and Clueless. Angel followed her and was soon asleep again with her warm, fuzzy back snug against Ellie's bare feet. Amazing what a comfort that was, Ellie thought.

At Helen's knock, Ellie and Angel jumped. Ellie went to the kitchen door to welcome Helen in while Angel sat calmly on the rug in front of the oven.

"Here, let me take some of that," Ellie said as she removed a bag of litter and a foil roasting pan from Helen's arms.

"Hmmmm, that certainly does look like Angel," Helen commented, staring at the cat. "And first thing, she needs a bath."

As if she knew what was coming, the cat twitched the tip of her tail and laid her ears back.

"Smart one, aren't you," Helen said, taking a small bottle of pet shampoo from a bag.

"You mean she understood you?"

"Well, she definitely understood something she didn't like the sound of," Helen replied.

Helen filled the kitchen sink with warm water while Ellie fetched a couple of bath towels from the upstairs bathroom. When Helen tried to pick Angel up, the little cat hissed at her.

"How about you try," she responded.

Ellie picked Angel up and gently placed her in the sink.

"Mrrrrooowwww."

"I know you don't like water," Ellie said in a soft, soothing tone. "But you'll feel better when you're clean."

"Mrrrooooowww."

Angel complained loudly through several shampoo and rinse cycles but, as a puzzled Helen noticed, she didn't try to bite or scratch Ellie. Dried, fluffed, and wrapped in towels, Angel was resettled on the rug in front of the oven where she contentedly dozed.

"That's almost certainly Angel," Helen said as she packed up the pet supplies. "Tom and the Maywood residents are going to be relieved to learn she survived that awful fire. I wonder how she was able to escape. From what I hear, that fire really roared through in a very short time."

"What I can't figure is how she ended up at my house," Ellie said. "It's quite a ways from Maywood House, and she's never even met me before."

Helen frowned. "Cats are strange and wondrous critters," she thoughtfully answered. "They seldom fail to surprise me."

Ellie put a pot of water to heat for tea while they cleaned up the kitchen and set up Angel's litter pan in the kitchen bathroom. They were seated at the kitchen table with plates of brownies and steaming mugs when Helen abruptly asked, "So, what do you think about Noel Hathaway?"

"He's easy to work with," Ellie responded. "I've been surprised because, when you think about it, coming from an exciting, high pressure daily in Detroit, you'd expect him to be too hard-edged for a small-town newspaper. It would feel to me like a comedown."

"Well, the talk around town is that he and Ed had this planned long ago but, because of Edith's breast cancer diagnosis, the changeover was sped up considerably," Helen mused.

This was gossip, something Ellie tried to avoid, but her curiosity overcame her natural reticence. "I suppose he has a family back in Detroit?"

"The scuttlebutt is he's divorced with adult children living in Upper Michigan," Helen said. "He came into the post office the other day to arrange for a personal box. What I can say with certainty is that Noel Hathaway has George Clooney eyes." As Ellie blushed, Helen grinned and added, "I see you've already noticed that."

"I didn't..., I mean I can't possibly..., errr," Ellie stammered.

Helen reached across the table and patted Ellie's hand. "It's okay. You're not the only woman in town who's noticed. I mean, he's a handsome hunk after all, and available."

Helen left after answering Ellie's questions about caring for Angel.

"You might want to have Vic the Vet check Angel over," Helen concluded. "She doesn't look as if she were experiencing any respiratory distress but with all that smoke, it would be a good idea to be sure."

Ellie watched Helen pull out of the driveway and waved. Turning back to the kitchen, she stared down at the drowsy cat. Helen answered all my questions except one: Why you happened to come to me, Ellie mused.

# CHAPTER 7

Ellie picked her way carefully across the rutted, frozen mess that once was Maywood House's immaculate front lawn. Ahead of her, she could see Thomas Wagner standing at the edge of the burned-out ruin, his shoulders hunched against the cold. The lovely old Victorian portion of the nursing home was now a tumbled mass of blackened timbers and smoldering embers. About half of the modern two-story expansion that had been built a few years before was also gone.

Ellie sighed and Thomas turned with a start. She was touched to see tears running down his cheeks. This interview was going to be an emotional one, something she hadn't anticipated from a seasoned professional administrator. Thomas brushed the tears away with brisk, jerky motions.

"Sorry, Ms. Franklin," he murmured. "I just can't believe it's gone. I loved this old place. I know, I'm just an employee but to be honest, it felt like home to me."

"It's Ellie, Thomas, and I know how you feel about Maywood," Ellie replied. "It was such a gracious, inviting place since Oscar Maywood willed it to the church. Thank goodness no one was seriously hurt."

Thomas shook his head. "Thank Angel. If she hadn't run through the house yowling at the top of her lungs, we wouldn't have known about the fire until it was too late. As it was, we were barely able to get everyone out safely.

I hear she showed up at your house. I was so happy to hear she was all right. She's a real heroine."

"Thomas, tell me what happened from your point of view," Ellie prompted, taking out her notepad.

Thomas rubbed his chin. His eyes turned back to the ruins. "I was at home with Marlene and the kids when the call came," he recalled. "We were all in bed at that hour of the night. It was all I could do to keep them home. They wanted to jump in the car and come with me. I drove here seeing the fire and black smoke despite the darkness, and I don't mind telling you I was terrified for the residents. It looked awful, and it was even worse when I arrived."

"Was everyone out by then?"

"No, and that's one of the reasons I was in a panic," Thomas added. "Thankfully, we had moved all the residents from the second floor of the original house and were using it for office space. All the residents had ground floor rooms in the newer wings with full accessibility. If anyone had still been in the old part, we would have had multiple fatalities. As it was, the firefighters were able to move the residents away from the fire and out of the untouched end of the wing."

Ellie shook her head. "That must have been a terrible moment, Thomas."

"It was. When I say Maybelle being loaded onto the medic helicopter with that oxygen mask over her face, I thought my heart would break," Thomas said, a tremor in his voice. "I hope they find who did this, and punish them severely. We haven't just lost a nursing home. Ellie, we've lost another one of Creekwood's wonderful landmarks. Oh, we can rebuild, even replicate the original to an extent, but somehow I feel it will never be the same again."

With a start, Ellie realized Thomas was referring to the twin barns. If he equated this tragic fire with the one in January, how much so would the rest of the community? Ellie couldn't think of anything else to ask at that point, and it was with relief that she saw Jason coming toward them with his photographic equipment in hand.

"Thomas, Jason is going to take photos of you here with the house as a backdrop," Ellie said. "I think I have everything I need but I'll give you a call if I have more questions after I start to write."

Thomas nodded in a distracted way, and walked along the edge of the caved-in foundation to meet Jason. Ellie tucked her notepad into her handbag and turned to trace her steps back to her car. Motion at the corner of her eye stopped her in her tracks. She turned to stare down into the smoky shambles and gasped. A shimmer coalesced slowly into the figure of a man. But not just any man, Ellie realized immediately. It was old Oscar Maywood, looking more chipper and suave than he ever had alive. The image blurred as he turned in a complete circle, hands on hips, surveying the destruction of his family home. Then with a visible start, he gazed straight up into Ellie's eyes.

"Oh, my goodness!" Ellie burst out.

Thomas and Jason stopped working on a pose and spun around.

"What's wrong, Ellie," Jason called out as the two began walking quickly toward her.

"Ah, ah...," Ellie stammered. Oscar disappeared. "I thought I saw something move down there," she managed to say.

Thomas and Jason peered down into the rubble. Ellie took a deep breath and stepped back from the crumbling edge of the basement.

"It probably was some of the debris settling," Jason said soothingly. "Things are going to shift as the heat dies down."

Jason patted her on the shoulder in what he must have thought was a reassuring manner. Thomas gave her an odd look before shrugging and walking off with Jason to finish the photo shoot. Ellie walked back to her car and sat inside, gazing back at the fire scene. Finally, she started the car and drove downtown to the Courier office where she spent the rest of the afternoon working on the story.

When Kirsten came in, Ellie stopped long enough to ask how the arson investigation was going.

"Well, the chief and mayor are keeping things pretty close to their chests," Kirsten answered with a disgusted look. "All they'll say is that the fire is under investigation and, because it is an open case, they can't discuss it with anyone, especially the press. Everyone is tippy toeing around more than usual."

Kirsten plunked down into her chair and poked the mouse hard enough to bring up her screen. Then she stared at the monitor for a moment before turning to face Ellie.

"You know, if I didn't know better, I would think they are already looking at someone for this arson and are afraid I'll find out who," Kirsten mused. "And that only makes me more curious because they aren't normally so closed-mouth. The police, fire department, and mayor are holding a meeting tonight but it's closed to the public, meaning I'm not welcome. Boy, I'd give anything to be there. Something is going down, I can feel it."

Ellie frowned. "Isn't that a violation of the open meetings act?"

"No, unfortunately in this case, it's not the city council that's meeting, it's the police investigators including the mayor, et al," Kirsten explained. "They aren't obligated, and even the council can close meetings if they are discussing legal or personnel matters. But Ellie, they aren't just being firm about this, they're actually paranoid. And that raises all kinds of red flags."

Kirsten opened a copy file on her computer and started writing. "Well, at least I can write what I know so far, and hope that someone, anyone, feels the need to pass on a tidbit or two on the investigation."

Home after a longer than usual work day, Ellie fed Angel and satisfied her hunger with a fried egg and ham sandwich. She took her knitting bag into the little sunroom where Jerry used to watch television and settled down in his favorite chair. After studying a new mitten pattern she had borrowed from Janelle, Ellie began the comfortable, familiar work of casting on stitches. After an hour or so, she felt herself nodding off.

"Ellie, be careful."

Ellie sat up, startled, and looked wildly around. No one was there, but she was absolutely positive she had heard Jerry's voice warning her to be careful. Angel was curled on the rug in front of the sliding doors, gazing out into the night with an expectant look on her feline face. Ellie looked down at her knitting and realized she had only completed about eight rows before falling asleep. With a snort of disgust, she resolutely picked up her needles and began working the next ribbing row.

"Murrrrrrow."

Ellie looked up and gasped. There, bold as life, stood Oscar Maywood in the middle of the sunroom with Angel curling around his legs and purring happily. Ellie dropped her knitting, cursed in an unladylike way, and scrambled to pick it up without letting the knitting needle slip out of the stitches.

Oscar chuckled. "Oh, my dear, I didn't mean to startle you like that."

"Oh, yes, you did!" Ellie shot back. Then she abruptly sat back in the chair and glared up at the dapper spirit of Oscar Maywood. "Go away, you're not real. This cannot be happening. There are no such things as ghosts. I shouldn't have eaten that fried egg. It was too greasy and now I'm having nightmares."

Oscar grimaced and grinned, "Oh, surely, Scrooge. It was a bit of undercooked potato, perhaps?"

Ellie stuffed her knitting back into the bag and prepared to rise. "Jerry warned me about you. And now you're still part of that dream, right?"

"Wrong. Jerry warned you to be careful, but not because of me," Oscar said. "That fire was deliberately set and meant to harm. Whoever did it is dangerous, and you are poking into things that could hurt you, too."

Ellie shot back, "You were in the house. Didn't you see who it was?"

With an exasperated groan, Oscar sat down on the plaid sofa where Ellie had always sat wrapped in a blanket to read or knit while Jerry watched his favorite sports. "I'm a spirit, not Houdini. I was in the new wing visiting with old Jacob Seversen when the fire started. I sent Angel to wake everyone up, but by the time I arrived at the back of the house, whoever had set the fire was gone."

Ellie gazed at Oscar with a perplexed expression. "What are you doing here, anyway?"

"You mean here in your home, or here at all," Oscar asked.

"Both."

"Ahhh, the intrepid reporter emerges," Oscar quipped, then held up a hand before Ellie could respond. "I'm still here because I have a mission to complete. I have waited for more than 20 years for this moment to fulfill my purpose. And I am in your home, Ellie because for some unearthly reason, you have been chosen to help me with that purpose."

"You're kidding."

"No, I'm not joking," Oscar replied, leaning forward and gazing earnestly into Ellie's face, accurately assessing her skepticism. "Like Jacob Marley in 'A Christmas Carol,' I am constrained to live amongst humanity and learn what I did not when I was alive. Worse, I was confined to my family home to do so until the fire freed me. Now I feel I must complete my purpose by bringing whoever destroyed my home to justice."

"You feel? You mean you don't know for certain?"

Oscar sighed. "No, it doesn't work quite that way. We spirits are not always sent back with specific instructions. We are expected to intuit what's needful, and if we are correct, we know. Of course, if we aren't right, we know that, too. It's a learning process, you see?"

"I promise I will never eat fried eggs for supper again," Ellie muttered. "Maybe the ham was spoiled."

Oscar shook his head sadly. "Ellie, we need to get past this credibility gap and get to work on finding out who set fire to Maywood House. He won't stop. We can deal with abstracts later, okay. Now, what are we going to do?"

Ellie didn't have to think, even for a moment. "You need to go to the police investigation meeting at City Hall right now," she exclaimed. "Kirsten said she believes they have a suspect and are being really evasive about it. We need to know what's going on so we can start putting all the facts together on our own."

"I can't go into a closed meeting!" Oscar replied. "That's illegal."

"So, who'd know? Am I the only one who can see you?"

Oscar looked thoughtful for a moment, then stilled as if listening to some unheard voice. "Very few who might be there would be able to see me," he answered. "Possibly only Thomas."

"Thomas Wagner, the administrator? He can see you?"

Oscar nodded. "He only saw me once, and I'm not certain who was more shocked, he or me."

"Why...?" Ellie started to ask, then stopped as she realized she didn't even honestly understand why she could see Oscar. They certainly didn't share any kind of connection that she recognized.

"Some are vulnerable to seeing spirits only at times while others are capable of seeing them all the time," Oscar said. "Don't ask because I truly don't understand it, either. It just seems to happen, and usually for a good reason. I know," he added when Ellie opened her mouth to question him. "I know, you hear about ghosts coming back for revenge. They are not coming from the same place, and that's all I'm going to be able to say on the subject."

Ellie sighed and reached for her knitting as a sort of comfort barrier against all the weirdness she was feeling. "So, are you going to the meeting?"

"Yes, I am," Oscar answered. "I'll be back as soon as I learn anything we can use."

As he faded away into the deep winter night outside the door, Ellie slumped back into the chair, buried her face in her hands, and moaned, "Boy, what a strange dream!"

Ellie set aside her knitting and rubbed her eyes. While it was still early, not quite 9:30, Ellie felt so tired she decided to get ready for bed. She was in the upstairs bathroom brushing her teeth when Oscar abruptly appeared in the mirror. Gasping and nearly choking on the toothbrush, she spun around and stared at him in exasperation.

"No, you're a dream," Ellie stated. "I was napping when you arrived and I refuse to believe you're real."

Oscar grunted, then grinned. "Well, you had better start believing, Ellie, because I have news for you."

Ellie slumped against the sink. "You mean I wasn't dreaming a while ago?"

"Nope," Oscar replied cheerfully. "I went to the meeting which, by the way, was very interesting. I didn't know they conducted business like that behind closed doors. What a bunch of gossips!"

"Business as usual," Ellie muttered. "So I'll play along. What have you learned about the arson investigation?"

"They think Noel did it," Oscar announced.

"What? What!"

"Yes, they went over a bunch of possible suspects. They double-checked Thomas' alibi and decided he could possibly have sneaked out while the family slept."

"Absurd."

"I agree," Oscar said. "Then they checked the list of all prior Maywood House employees to see if any of them had reason to be disgruntled, as the mayor put it."

"The mayor was at the police investigation meeting?" Ellie mused. "That doesn't sound right."

"And they started investigating the families of the residents to see if any one of them inherits a lot of money or valuables," Oscar continued.

"Now that makes perfect sense but how did Noel get on the suspect list?"

"His honor pointed out that Creekwood had never experienced an arson until he arrived," Oscar said. "And then they all speculated that, because he was such a big-time, big-city editor, perhaps he felt he needed a little more excitement to help sell papers."

"Now that is ridiculous," Ellie fumed. "Even the notion that anyone would put helpless people in jeopardy for a headline is, well, it's just unbelievable."

"You know how people are in small communities, Ellie. They'll believe anything of a person they consider an outsider."

"We have to warn Noel," Ellie exclaimed.

She turned to the sink, spat out the toothpaste she still had in her mouth, gave it a quick rinse, and stuffed her toothbrush in its holder. She reached for her cell phone but Oscar stopped her.

"Ellie, I think you need to tell Kirsten first," he suggested.

"Why?"

"Well, if word gets out that someone is sharing information from a closed meeting, she'll get blamed because she's the one who will write the story," Oscar pointed out. "She will need to prove where she was so they don't believe she was snooping in City Hall."

"Hmmm, you're right," Ellie said, punching Kirsten's cell phone number into her phone.

"Kirsten? Oh, good, you answered," Ellie began. "I have information from a, what do they call it, an unimpeachable source that the police suspect Noel of starting the fire."

Ellie pulled the phone away from her ear at Kirsten's loud, "What?"

"I can't tell you where I heard this," Ellie continued, thinking Kirsten most likely wouldn't believe her if she did. "They think Noel is out to grab attention and sell papers. In fact, it was your favorite Creekwood politician, Mayor Larson, who brought it up."

"Oh, my God," Kirsten breathed.

"Kirsten, where are you?"

"Oh," Kirsten hesitated slightly. "I'm out at the Lazy River Lodge having a drink with a friend," she said, a bit too casually.

Was Kirsten out with Noel, Ellie wondered, then shook off the thought and said, "I'm going to call Noel right now and warn him."

"No, no, don't do that, Ellie," Kirsten quickly interrupted. "If you tell him, he and everyone else will wonder who your source is. To protect your source, I'll tell him but I won't mention where I got that information. That way, you and the source are protected. And if there's any fallout, it lands on me which it would have anyway."

"Well, if you say so," Ellie reluctantly agreed.

She filled Kirsten in on the other investigative information, and said goodnight.

"What's bothering you?"

"Kirsten was kind of cagey about who she was having a drink with, Oscar," Ellie said. "What if it was Noel?"

"I can find out right now."

Ellie thought about it for a moment. "No, that feels like an invasion of Kirsten's privacy. Much as I'd like to satisfy my curiosity, I am uncomfortable with asking you to spy on her. Let's stick to solving this arson."

"Good for you, Ellie," Oscar beamed. "I'm beginning to understand why you were chosen to help me. I always did like you. When I complained about the kids, you were straightforward and honest with me. We're going to make a great team."

Later, as Ellie lay in bed staring up at the ceiling and wondering if she was going insane, a big grin slowly slid across her face.

"I know I may be cracking up, but all I have to say right now is, 'Go team!,'" she murmured as she finally really fell asleep.

# CHAPTER 8

Noel was upset and for good reason, Ellie thought as she focused intently on her computer monitor to avoid catching his eye. He stormed around the newsroom like an avenging force while Kirsten tried to reason with him.

"You can't just march into the police department and start shouting," Kirsten said in a calming tone. "In fact, I think it would be better if they didn't know we are aware of their attention."

Noel stopped abruptly and stared at Kirsten. "Okay, I'll buy that. We'll tell them we know enough without telling them we know it all. Let them wonder and squirm. Put in the parts about investigating past employees and family members. Say they are looking at other possible suspects. Hint that some may be surprising and disturbing."

"And what are you going to do?" Kirsten added.

"Well, the bad news is I don't have an alibi," he replied, then added emphatically,. "I was home, in bed… alone."

Ellie felt a flush building, warmth that flooded through her and turned her face rosy. She mentally kicked herself. That sounded as if it were meant for me to hear, she thought, then brushed away the idea that Noel cared about what she thought of him. Ridiculous, she scolded herself as she sorted through the latest batch of PSAs with determination. She felt Kirsten's eyes on her and looked up.

"He's gone," Kirsten stated with a grin. She held up a finger as Ellie started to protest. "A person would need to be totally numb not to feel the electricity between the two of you. It literally has my hair standing on end. I can hear it crackling."

Ellie pushed the PSAs aside and sighed. "Kirsten, I've been widowed less than two months."

"So, what does time have to do with feelings?" Kirsten demanded. "Feelings are never right or wrong, they just are. I admit this isn't good timing for either of you, what with Noel being suspected of arson and your recent loss. You don't have to do anything about the attraction except try to deny it. That only makes things worse."

Ellie thought about what Kirsten had said as she drove home. Pulling into the driveway, she decided that it was okay to acknowledge her attraction to Noel, at least to herself. That was how she honestly felt. But, it was what she could do about her feelings that was most important, and right now that was going to be pretty much nothing. Young as she was in years, Kirsten was refreshingly savvy when it came to insights into relationships, and Ellie silently blessed her for her advice.

That decided, she walked into the kitchen to find Oscar seated at the table, with Angel curled up in her usual spot in front of the oven. Resignedly, Ellie set her purse on the counter and sighed.

"I just popped in to tell you that the police chief invited Noel to come in and talk about the fire," Oscar said.

"Is he there now?"

"Yes, he's there right now."

"That is so absurd," Ellie fumed.

"Don't worry, Ellie," Oscar advised in a soothing tone. "I have a feeling they won't be looking at Noel as a suspect for very long."

Ellie filled the kettle, put it on to heat, and pulled her favorite mug out of the cupboard. She paused and gazed over her shoulder at Oscar.

"What do you mean, you have a feeling? Do you know what's going to happen ahead of time?"

"There are things I am given to know," Oscar replied. "Not all things, however. It feels like intuition more than conviction. A hunch, you might call it. I just know that things are going to change for Noel very soon."

Thoughtfully, Ellie dropped a chai teabag into the bright green mug and opened the refrigerator to take out the cream.

"Oscar, you just said you popped in. Where do you go when you're not here?"

"You mean here in your home or here in the real world," Oscar asked. At her nod to the second choice, he added, "I can't say."

"What do you mean, you can't say?"

"I literally cannot say. I know, of course, but I am constrained from saying it."

"Why?"

It was Oscar's turn to look thoughtful. "I suppose it is because human beings are better off not knowing. Remember faith, hope, and charity? Think what would happen to faith if people were absolutely certain of heaven and hell. If they knew for sure, where hope would fit into their lives? Or charity even. Why give to those in need when you know they will have a better place to go."

"Hmmmm," Ellie poured water into the mug and gently dipped the tea bag up and down. "Can you tell me if Jerry is there?"

"I can and he is," Oscar beamed.

"Is he okay?" Ellie whispered as she sat down at the table, steaming mug in hand. "Am I going to see his spirit, too?"

"He's more than okay, Ellie, and that's all I can tell you," Oscar said. "As for seeing his spirit, Jerry has no earthly issues to resolve. He was a good man, so there is no reason for him to return."

Ellie blew on the tea and took a tentative sip. "You sort of answered my question, you know."

"Yes, I sort of did that, didn't I," Oscar mused. "But I was allowed to, so it must be all right."

Ellie started to ask another question when her cell phone rang. Answering it, she heard Kirsten's breathless, excited voice.

"Ellie, you need to come immediately, Someone has set fire to the Lazy River Lodge!"

Ellie dumped her tea in the sink, grabbed her coat and purse from the back of a stool, and rushed out to her car. Lazy River Lodge lay on a pine-edged meadow about a half-mile south of Creekwood. The timber and stone lodge with its hotel, restaurants, indoor swimming pool bar, roller skating rink, shops and theater was a magnet for families wanting to escape city living for a weekend or more. The lodge drew its guests from across the Midwest, but most came in from Chicago, Milwaukee, and Madison.

As Ellie drove south toward what she could now see as a spiraling column of smoke, she heard the whop-whop of a helicopter. Looking up through her windshield, she saw it zoom overhead and circle, WGN in large letters on its underside.

"Oh, my," she mumbled. "We've really hit the big time this time."

Ellie parked as close as she could, and hiked uphill to the lodge's main parking area where she was blocked by yellow crime scene tape. Kirsten appeared out of nowhere and pulled her under the tape with a cautionary finger to her lips.

"They're too busy to bother with us unless we really get in the way," she whispered. "Just stick close to me."

The two women edged along the front of the crowd that was gathering. Ellie turned to look at the lodge and gasped in awe. Flames rose more than 30 feet into the darkening sky and lit the scene with a lurid, surrealistic glow. As heat caused windows to burst outward, Ellie could see the white-hot fire eating its way through the hotel wing where more than 200 rooms clustered around a warren of hallways.

The original lodge had been built in the mid-1930s, starting with a gas station. Its owner, Maxwell Harris, proved himself a savvy businessman who saw the potential in bringing wealthy guests to the bucolic Wisconsin countryside for rest, relaxation and business. As his clientele grew, so did the lodge, added to in rambling segments that reflected the needs and interests of its visitors. Ellie had heard that most of the lodge was built with reclaimed lumber from other old buildings, barns, and even railroad ties. One person had described the lodge's underside as a vast crawl space punctuated with rotting wood, a firestarter's dream and a firefighter's nightmare. Now it looked as it both had been realized.

Staring into the fierce flames, Ellie swore she saw something, or someone, move inside the lodge's frightful blaze. She gasped out loud and stumbled, drawing Kirsten's attention.

"What?"

"I thought I saw someone inside the building," she blurted out before she could stop.

"Oh, my God, we have to tell Chief Olson," Kirsten replied, tugging on Ellie's coat sleeve.

Ellie balked. "It may have been my imagination," Ellie temporized.

"We still have to tell him," Kirsten insisted. Turning toward the fire, she added, "Although how someone could be alive in all that, seems unlikely."

An unwilling Ellie followed Kirsten toward a tight knot of firefighters grouped near an aerial fire truck. Above, two firefighters supported a thick hose between them as water cannoned onto the lodge's roof. It had taken only a second or two for Ellie to realize that the human figure she had glimpsed in the flames must have been Oscar. Because she couldn't very well tell Kirsten this, she shuffled along behind as Kirsten rushed up to the firefighters. Just as Kirsten opened her mouth, the entire roof of the lodge's hotel section collapsed, sending a vast cloud of fiery cinders into the sky. With a groan, the second floor fell onto the first which in turn folded into itself and then into the crawl space.

"Good lord!" the fire chief exclaimed. Cupping his hands around his mouth, he shouted up to the two firefighters aloft on the aerial, "Matt, Joe! Can you see Phil and Dave?"

"Not anymore!" one of the men yelled down.

The chief didn't have to say another word. Firefighters swarmed from every direction, all headed straight for the worst part of the fire. At the same time, the men on the aerial centered the water on the area where the two firefighters were last seen. While Ellie and Kirsten stood watching, numb with fear, Josh sidled up beside them, cradling his camera in his hands. Kirsten saw him out of the corner of her eye and turned.

"Josh," she murmured, "take photos of the crowd right away. Start at one end and overlap them so you don't miss a single person. It's important."

Josh's eyes widened as he understood what Kirsten really meant. Methodically, he began taking shots at the crowd, covering his actions with occasional frames of the fire. After a few minutes, he casually meandered further along the taped off area, shooting both fire and spectators. Finally, he leaned against a tree as if resting and took more photos of those farther away. The grim expression on his face pretty much said it all.

Meanwhile, the firefighters were frantically digging through the debris at the center of the collapsed hotel, seemingly heedless of the scorching heat, flames, and smoke. Finally, a shout from one signaled that they had found at least one of the two men.

"Here! Here!" brought every firefighter in the immediate area climbing over fallen timbers and burnt stone.

"Hurry!" the fire chief screamed. "That wall is about to give way. Get them out! Get them out!"

The firefighters' actions intensified as they struggled to pull burning rubble off their colleagues.

"Got 'em!" one yelled.

The firefighters lifted the two downed men and dashed out of harm's way just as the wall crumbled and fell. One firefighter who was slightly behind the others seemed to fly through the air and land hard on the frozen ground. He sat there, dazed and unmoving until two others rushed back to grab and propel him to safety. An ambulance that had been standing by pulled up and EMTs exploded out of it. Within moments, the three injured firefighters were gently laid on gurneys, soot-smeared faces covered with oxygen masks.

"Phil, how are you, man," one firefighter asked.

Phil pulled the mask away long enough to say, "Broken ankle. Maybe broken ribs. Someone pulled us out."

"Yeah, man, it was us," the firefighter replied.

"No, before you guys got to us," Phil gasped.

But before he could continue, an EMT firmly placed the mask back over his nose and mouth. "Talk later," he said as the ambulance doors closed.

"What about Dave?" the firefighter called.

"Broken shoulder, bruised ribs, sprained knee," was the hasty reply before the ambulance pulled away, lights flashing and siren revving up.

Kirsten turned to Ellie with an odd expression. Ellie cringed inside, frantically wondering how she could dodge the subject. Noel inadvertently came to her rescue.

"Holy smoke," he said, then grimaced. "Are there any fatalities?"

"We're not sure yet," Kirsten answered, giving Ellie another quizzical look. "Two firefighters were injured and are on their way to UW-Madison Hospital. It doesn't appear to be life threatening. But we don't know if everyone staying inside the lodge made it out."

Noel shook his head. "Bad and getting worse," he remarked.

"And where were you while all this was happening," a gruff voice behind them demanded.

They turned to find Fire Chief Olson standing behind them, wearing a suspicious glare.

"Why don't you ask Chief McGrath?" Noel said. "I just spent the past hour-and-a-half being raked over the coals, so to speak."

Chief McGrath sauntered up to the group and nodded to Noel. "At ease, John. Noel was in my office when the fire started."

But the fire chief was undeterred. "Where were you before that?"

Noel frowned. "I drove to Madison late this morning to visit my sister-in-law at UW-Madison Hospital," he replied. "I returned to find Chief McGrath parked in my driveway."

Olson's grim expression softened. "How is Edith?"

"She's so-so right now," Noel answered. "I'm actually more worried about Ed. He's barely holding it together."

As the three men continued their conversation, Kirsten pulled Ellie aside.

"They must think the fires were started with incendiary devices," Kirsten whispered. "Otherwise, why would they question where Noel was in the hours right before the fires started."

Ellie whispered back, "But that would mean the person who started the fires was nowhere nearby when they began. That's going to make finding him or her a lot tougher, isn't it?"

The women gazed at each other, each wondering how this little piece of information fit into the mystery. Ellie pulled her reporter's pad from her purse, saying, "I'm going to work the crowd. Maybe I'll hear or see something."

Kirsten nodded. "And I'm going to interview those firefighters who pulled Dave and Phil from the rubble.

There's something odd about what they said. And about how that last firefighter literally flew out of harm's reach."

Ellie didn't respond. She knew full well how those firefighters were saved from more serious injury. Oscar had been there. She had no doubt at all that it had been Oscar's invisible hands that had saved their lives. And it had been Oscar she had glimpsed through the flames, walking the blazing hallways of the lodge searching for victims. Bless him, she thought. Oscar was more than making up for all that lost time.

Walking the tape line, Ellie had no trouble finding more than enough material for her feature story. Lazy River Lodge had long been a landmark in Creekwood, and was also one of its major employers. Nearly everyone had worked at the lodge in some capacity from their mid-teens to retirement jobs. Bell boys, valets, chefs, waiters and bus boys, maids, maintenance, clerks, bartenders, so many positions had been filled by Creekwood residents that it would have been more challenging to find anyone who was not connected to the lodge in some way. After more than an hour, Ellie resolutely closed her note pad knowing she would get phone calls from those she had not spoken with directly, wanting their views and news known.

Back in her car, Ellie flipped the overhead light on and scanned through her notes. Nothing jumped out at her. She shook her head disgustedly. This wasn't a movie where the heroine gets a clue without even trying, and then solves the crime on her own. Nearly getting herself killed in the process, Ellie reminded herself with a rueful grin. Reality might bite but on the other hand, it was a lot safer as a rule.

Ellie started the car and turned to check traffic behind her. From the corner of her eye, she saw a shadow move and froze. Someone was skulking through one of the parking lots. As she stared out into the darkness, the figure ran from tree to tree and then took cover behind a hedge. She started to put the car into park and get out, then thought the better of it. No one else was in sight. It might just be some kid sneaking out of his house for a closer look at the fire. Perfectly innocent or perhaps not, but Ellie instantly realized she was too vulnerable outside the car and alone.

Instead, she put the car into drive and heard the reassuring clunk of the door locks. Easing out into the roadway, she drove ever so slowly down the block and made a U-turn at the first possible right. Accelerating, she zipped past the parking lot where she had seen the skulker and turned left. Then she turned around in a driveway and went back to the intersection. This should have put her ahead of the skulker if he or she were headed toward the fire. Parking just short of the intersection, Ellie killed the headlights and watched intently.

Her intuition was rewarded. Moments later, she saw movement to her left. Ellie sat poised with her hand on the light switch. As the dark figure drifted into the open directly in front of her, Ellie pulled the switch, flooding the yard with light. A slight person, perhaps a young teen, froze open-mouthed for a split second before dashing across the gravel lot and disappearing into some bushes. Etched in Ellie's memory was the image of a short, slender person with close-cropped dark hair. It could have been a boy or a girl, Ellie thought, possibly in the middle school age range. And, she added, more than likely a fugitive from parents who had sternly forbade going out of the house to check out the fire. Still, she jotted down what she had seen in her note pad, and then drove home.

# CHAPTER 9

Ellie gazed out of her kitchen window at the drab March day and sighed. Saturday mornings had always been one of her favorite times. Though it was not a workday, she and Jerry had still awakened early. With a fresh-brewed pot of coffee and the prospect of a hearty pancake brunch, they had settled in the sunroom watching the birds, squirrels and chipmunks and sharing small talk. Now the silence was deafening and the thought of pancakes no longer held the same appeal.

When Janelle rapped on the back door, Ellie was relieved. She opened the door with a smile and gestured for Janelle to come in while she gathered up her coat and purse.

"What, no breakfast?" Janelle said, taking a deep breath but smelling only coffee.

"I thought I'd save the space for a really good lunch," Ellie replied as they locked up the house and climbed into Janelle's car. "So what's Don up to this morning?"

Janelle laughed. "He said he was going to clean out the garage. I suspect he'll get as far as sorting and scraping down the flower pots for the patio. I've never seen him more anxious for spring to come."

"I can relate," Ellie nodded. "I'm so happy you suggested going to Cambridge today. It's just what I need.

A short road trip, great shopping, and good food that I didn't cook."

Janelle chuckled. "Amen to that."

Cambridge had long been a go-to favorite with folks across south central Wisconsin. The small but lively town had its own personality and appealed to a wide sector of visitors from families to seniors on day trips. With its Amish, artisan and antique shops, trendy restaurants and its biggest draws, the Rowe Pottery Works and Cambridge Stoneware, the town had a lot to offer. It didn't hurt that just outside of town, Lake Ripley drew vacationers, boaters, campers and fishermen to its lovely woodland shores in the summer. And on this cloudy, chill March morning, Ellie couldn't think of a better way to spend time with a good friend. She settled back in her seat and sighed deeply.

"Rough week," Janelle said. It wasn't a question but an acknowledgment.

"Yeah. Three suspicious fires within two months and only pure luck that no one died. I've only worked in a newspaper office for a couple of months but I already can't imagine what it would be like to be a reporter in a major city. How on earth do they handle the stress? How can they stand the way it effects people?"

"I don't know, maybe it's easier in big cities where things are less personal," Janelle offered.

"Kirsten says hard news reporting requires a fire in the belly," Ellie mused.

"What does she mean by that?"

Ellie thought for a moment. "I think she was referring to being assertive about finding the truth, and not letting anything get in the way of digging deep," she finally replied. "Lately, there's been more than enough fire around without adding to the heat."

"Do the police have any leads?"

"Not that I am aware of. Right now, they are working on theories and suspicions."

Janelle glanced over at Ellie. "Like Noel Hathaway?"

Ellie straightened up in her seat. "Right. As if that wasn't the most absurd thing I've heard," Ellie responded indignantly.

Gazing out the window at the dreary country landscape, Ellie didn't see the little smile that crossed Janelle's face as she listened to Ellie defend Noel. The rest of the drive to Cambridge passed in companionable quiet.

"Okay, where do we begin?" Janelle asked as her car slowed at the city limits.

"We might as well hit the pottery shops and get it over with," Ellie grinned. "I can never get through them without buying something."

Janelle parked on Cambridge's main street where the two pottery shops faced each other across the traffic. Ellie led the way to Cambridge Stoneware where occasionally a visitor might catch owner Jim Rowe in his workshop. After browsing through all the new spring designs, Ellie picked out an American salt-glazed butter crock with a lid.

"What are you going to use that for?"

"Not butter," Ellie replied. "Probably tea bags. Besides, it matches the canister set Jerry bought me two Christmases ago. I can serve candies and olives and pickles and other stuff in it, too."

Across the street, Ellie and Janelle were instantly drawn to Rowe Pottery Works' newest offering. A sweet blue snail balanced precariously on a slender green blade of grass above a delicate pink flower. Ellie bought a quiche pan with the design while Janelle finally settled on a small vase.

"I really missed our annual Christmas shopping trip with Don and Jerry," Janelle commented.

"Me, too," Ellie murmured, tears welling in her eyes. "You just don't realize all the meaningful things you have to let go. It's hard. I suppose this year is going to be a constant succession of things lost forever for the first time."

"And on that note, let's go eat lunch," Janelle said brightly in an effort to lighten the mood again.

The friends settled comfortably at a table in one of Cambridge's popular restaurants. Just as Ellie was digging her fork into a huge platter of pasta, she heard a woman's voice behind her saying, "...and my neighbor's husband is a psychologist. He says those fires in Creekwood might have been set by a serial pyromaniac."

Ellie and Janelle froze, Janelle with a spoon full of baked potato soup almost in her mouth. She lowered it slowly, and they gazed at each other, eyebrows raised.

"I've never heard of such a thing," another woman was saying behind them.

"Well," the first continued, "he said they start out as abused children who play with matches and also torment animals. Then they progress to starting fires so they can watch the firefighters respond. And if they don't get help, they escalate to deliberately setting fires in occupied buildings so they can watch both the firefighters and people die."

"That's awful!" the other women exclaimed.

"Yeah, it is, and what's to prevent this pervert from coming to any one of the other towns nearby like Cambridge and setting fires here, too," the first pointed out.

The waitress's arrival with the women's bill interrupted their discussion. As Ellie and Janelle waited silently, the women left the table. Ellie sat back and set her fork down with a clunk.

"I wish I hadn't heard that," Ellie murmured.

"Me, too, but if it is true, our hearing about it wouldn't make a difference," Janelle said. "It does sound a bit far-fetched, though, doesn't it? Like some thriller-killer novel."

"I'm skeptical, too. It sounds like a plot on CSI to me," Ellie agreed. "So many television crime programs focus on serial killers these days. And yet, from what I've heard and read, true serial killers are extremely rare in any case. Pyromaniacs would logically represent an even smaller percentage of that statistic."

Janelle raised another spoonful of soup to her lips, then paused. "Yeah, and what are the odds we'd have one living in Creekwood that we didn't know about? I mean, you could count the number of families that have moved in during the past year on the fingers on one hand. It would almost have to be one of us."

Ellie sighed. "Now that's a disquieting thought. Oh, please!"

"What?"

"At least finish one bite of that soup," Ellie replied with a grin. "It's nearly made it into your mouth five times already."

Janelle, who had finally shoved the spoon into her mouth, sputtered and covered it with a hand. They burst out laughing, and afterward finished their lunch and shopped in a leisurely manner without the subject of pyromania coming up again.

Back home that evening, Ellie set a plate of reheated pasta from lunch on the kitchen table and went into the living room to fetch her laptop. While it booted up, she poured a glass of rose wine and pulled a new notepad and pencil from the drawer. Chewing thoughtfully on a mouthful of pasta, she keyed the word pyromania into the search box and hit enter. She wasn't surprised with the zillions of references that popped up.

Alternating eating with writing, Ellie wrote down everything she found that seemed to fit what was happening in Creekwood. Then she began assembling the information into columns labeled facts, traits, and opportunities.

"And we are doing what?"

Ellie was proud that she didn't even flinch when Oscar popped into the kitchen. Angel greeted him with a soft, drawn-out meow and wrapped herself around his legs. Briefly, Ellie wondered if either one could actually feel the other.

"I'm profiling our firestarter," Ellie answered.

"Oho! You mean like in Criminal Minds?"

Ellie frowned. "That TV show wasn't even on when you were still alive," she replied.

"Yeah, but when you are sitting up with a friend in a nursing home all night, there's not much on TV except crime investigation reruns."

"There's that," Ellie agreed.

Oscar leaned over the table and scanned down through her notes.

"So, what we have here may lead us to believe we're looking for an older teenaged boy, right?"

Ellie thought about it for a moment, then said, "Maybe. According to these sources, 90 percent of pyromanics are male. Individually, they may be antisocial, are truant from school a lot, run away from home, are considered delinquent, may have ADHS or have been neglected or sexually abused. On the other hand, it says pyromania may be simply a matter of temperament."

"Oh, my, that's awful," Oscar remarked.

"And then we would have to take into consideration environmental influences such as living in a household without much of a father figure, or something called parental psychopathology."

"Ewww, I don't like the sound of that. What is it, exactly?"

Ellie chewed on the eraser end of her pencil. "I'm not exactly sure, and I'm fairly sure I don't really want to know."

"Is there more?"

"Yes. It says the firestarter may also have a record of past crimes including vandalism and non-violent sexual assault," Ellie muttered.

"So we should be looking at teen boys?"

"Maybe."

"Why maybe?"

Ellie shook her head. "If no one realizes that the child has a problem and gets help, he grows up into an adult pyromaniac. That means every single man in Creekwood and the surrounding countryside could be one."

It was Oscar's turn to sigh. "So now what? Where do we begin?"

Ellie shut down the laptop and finished the last sip of her wine. "I'm going to research a lot closer to home, starting with one of my more reliable sources."

On Sunday morning, Ellie entered the church sanctuary and deliberately chose a seat in the pew that, in the past, she privately had always called Widow's Row. If anyone wanted to take the pulse of the Creekwood community, this was as good a place as any to start. The good widows, and divorcees if truth be told, spent a lot of time out and about with friends and family. Collectively, they could provide a fairly thorough knowledge of anything odd or out of character within the close confines of the community.

Ellie sat in companiable silence through the service, then joined the knot of single women outside in the parking lot. As she had hoped, the first thing discussed was where they all were going to gather for lunch. And she was ready when one of them invited her to join them.

The little clutch of women, seven in all, regathered at the Atrium Café and Bakery, situated on the riverbank just outside the downtown area. The cafe, with its elegant glassed-in atrium addition, occupied the first floor of a historic ginger brick two-story building decked in delicate gingerbread trim. Once a home, the cozy café was a favorite with the ladies who flocked to its charming environment for elegant teas, dainty sandwiches and salads, quiches, innovative soups and scrumptious desserts. The Atrium was Wisconsin's answer to a genuine Texas teahouse, and for good reason.

Its owners, the Olmsteads, had spent many years in the San Antonio area while the man of the house served in the military. When he had retired five years ago, the family had moved to Creekwood and purchased the brick house. The family, including two teens, had moved in upstairs. Within a year, the Atrium had opened its doors complete with the lacy glass and wood addition, to the delight of the entire community. The women had made it the go-to place for luncheons, receptions, and birthday and anniversary celebrations or just because they loved the delicious bakery and menu items that the Atrium had to offer.

Ellie paused just inside the doorway, and gazed along a gleaming glass display case lined with shelves. Just the aroma of fresh-baked cookies was enough to start her mouth watering without the sight of all those cakes, pies, breads, donuts and sweet rolls. She followed the girls, who were in turn following a sullen-faced young woman into the atrium portion of the café. Here, sunlight poured through the spotless glass panels, belying the March chill outside. Ferns and flowers hung in large baskets overhead while garlands of deep green ivy with tiny white lights and flowers were woven around pillars. The tables, set with crisp white linens and vases of fresh greenery, were especially inviting.

Nibbling on a wedge of classic quiche Lorraine, a green salad splashed with Mandarin orange and almond dressing and a cup of creamy pumpkin soup, Ellie waited for the right moment to bring up the fires. It didn't take long. Before she had eaten half of the plate before her, one of her dining companions, Lorna Johnson, said, "So, Ellie, you've been covering these fires. Who do you think is starting them?"

Ellie lowered her fork reluctantly. "Personally, I don't know what to think, much less who."

Lorna pressed on. "Don't you guys have a pretty good idea who's responsible?"

"No, we're as much in the dark as you. The fire inspectors and police have been closed-mouthed about it. And to be truthful, I have heard a few rumors but nothing credible about who might be responsible."

"Ellie," another woman began tentatively. "Are you writing an article about us?"

Ellie shook her head. "No, not at all. I'm just very concerned as you are about the fires, and the fact that the authorities are having trouble finding the person responsible."

"Oh, good," the woman replied

The atmosphere around the table relaxed markedly. Oh, dear, Ellie thought, please don't become afraid to talk to me. That would be awful, a side to newspaper reporting she hadn't dreamed existed. Nor did she continue to probe. A few subtle comments here and there during the luncheon would pretty much guarantee that she would start getting phone calls with little tips and a lot of gossip. They would not come right out in public and point a finger, but they would share their information during the relative privacy of a telephone call or email. Ellie bided her time and hoped she had struck a nerve with at least one of the women, all of whom spent a great deal of time volunteering throughout the community. If there was a hint or a snippet, they would eventually pass sit on.

As the unsmiling young woman who had seated them arrived with a tray of desserts, Ellie glanced up. A shock of recognition shot through her. She immediately dropped her gaze to the table and hoped the girl had not noticed. It made no sense at all, but something about the girl rattled her. Even though she had not clearly seen the person's face, Ellie was nearly 100-percent certain that the teen passing around the desserts was the figure in black she had glimpsed skulking in the parking lots around the resort during the fire.

The young waitress served the dessert, moving around the table, and saving Ellie for last. She put Ellie's dish down a bit hard, causing a plunk that momentarily turned a couple of heads. Ellie and the teen made direct eye contact, and then the waitress lowered her eyes and said, "Excuse me, Mrs. Franklyn."

Ellie spent the rest of the luncheon wondering what that was all about. As she rose to go pay her check, the waitress approached the table with a white bakery sack. Setting it down in front of Ellie, she picked up Ellie's check and wrote something on it.

"I forgot to put these scones you ordered on the bill," she said, and hurried away.

Ellie stared after her, frowning. She hadn't ordered scones. Glancing around, she saw a few of the other women had noticed and may have overheard. They might know I didn't order these as well, Ellie guessed. Someone else was at the cash register so Ellie didn't have a chance to ask. She paid the bill, which did not include the scones and walked to her car. Behind the wheel, she opened the bag and pulled out the receipt. On it was written not "Thank you" or "Have a nice day" but a telephone number.

# CHAPTER 10

The instant Ellie walked into the Creekwood Courier offices Monday morning, the electricity in the atmosphere hit her like a hot wind. It wasn't just Martha's grim expression or the fact that Noel's office door was open. Stepping into the editorial area, she saw Kirsten and Jason already at their computer terminals, Kirsten with the phone headset clamped tightly between her shoulder and one ear while she keyed in data with flying fingers. Neither of them looked up or greeted her.

Ellie settled into her desk and sorted through the morning's last-minute PSAs. Once she finished inputting them and sent the file to Noel, she began opening articles to copy-edit.

"Oh, my god!" she blurted out.

The top article was a preliminary report on a huge fire the night before in Jefferson, a larger town not far from Creekwood. This time, fire had not only destroyed a century-old church but also had claimed victims. Four little girls who had been attending a Brownie Scout meeting were hospitalized, three were in fair condition and one critical. By the grace of God and the heroic efforts of a troop of older Boy Scouts who were also meeting at the church, the other little girls had been led to safety. Two of the boys had suffered injuries and were treated by paramedics at the scene before being transported to the

UW-Madison Hospital emergency room for treatment of burns and smoke inhalation.

Kirsten ended her call and turned to Ellie. "We didn't call you out because this broke out around 8 p.m., it was out of town, and there was no need to involve you yet. It's just awful. Those poor, beautiful little girls. It makes me sick to think of them innocently going into that church basement for what is one of the best parts of childhood, and then this happens."

Ellie shook her head as tears formed in her eyes. "I cannot believe someone would do such a thing, Kirsten. I did some research online about pyromania and, even with expert explanations, I still don't understand why."

Kirsten nodded, adding, "And on top of that, Jefferson lost one of its historic churches. It was a painful blow to the entire community. And worse, it is a sign that this crazy isn't going to limit his madness to the Creekwood area. That's really scary because now the police and fire departments all over the area will have to be on constant alert, not just here."

By mid-morning, Kirsten had received word that the critically injured little girl had died. Ellie stayed long past her usual Monday schedule, helping update stories and copy-editing cutlines. Jason's photos were incredibly intense. In one scene, flames rose high in the dark sky framing the church's steeple and illuminating the firefighters clustered around manning hoses. Another was a close-up of one of the Boy Scouts being treated before transport. A third focused on the church pastor, his wife and children huddled in the fire-shadowed darkness, tears streaming down their faces.

When it all was put together and sent on to the printers, Ellie could barely find enough energy to put her jacket on and walk out of the Courier office. As she passed Noel's office, he called out to her to come in for a moment. Standing in front of his desk, she waited to hear what Noel had to say.

"Ellie, sit down, you look exhausted," Noel exclaimed.

Ellie sank into a chair and sighed.

"It's not physical," she murmured. "But the thought that someone I might know is responsible for this tragedy is almost more than I can bear. And if I look tired, I can't imagine how you, Kirsten and Jason feel. You've been working all night."

"I know, I feel the same way," Noel commiserated. "It's different from working at a newspaper in Detroit, mainly because we rarely reported on criminals we could know personally. It makes things all the more painful."

Noel was silent, staring out of the window at Creekwood's Main Street. Then he pulled his attention back to Ellie.

"And I confess I'm worried about you," he said.

Ellie frowned. "Worried about me? Why?"

"You live alone. With the kind of stories we are planning to publish, we all could become targets for someone's anger," Noel replied. "Is there someone who can stay with you at night? A friend or neighbor?"

Ellie thought for a moment. With Oscar lurking about and Angel hanging out, she was hardly alone but she couldn't very well tell Noel that. Instead, she pointed out that Kirsten lived alone as well, and Jason had an apartment over his parent's garage, which meant he was essentially alone also. So, too, was Noel.

"I mean it, Ellie. See if you can find someone to be with you, especially at night," Noel stressed, his face set in serious lines. "Let me know that you have worked on this by our meeting tomorrow afternoon. Promise me?"

Holding back another sigh, this time one of exasperation, Ellie just nodded. She got up and collected her purse.

"I promise to work on it."

By the time she settled into her car and backed out of her parking place, Ellie was totally wrung out. The last thing she needed was someone trying to shepherd her at this late stage in her life. She stopped by Janelle's house to share the horrific news, and get a much-needed hug.

"I just heard," Janelle said as she seated Ellie at the kitchen table and poured tea. Pushing a plate of lemon bars closer to Ellie, Janelle sighed. "You know, it's not something you expect, living in a small town like Creekwood. Maybe that's why it hits us so hard."

Ellie sipped the hot, fragrant tea and nodded. "So true. But the world has changed so much since you and I moved here. I guess it was too much to ask that all the craziness and violence would pass us by. I'm afraid of what this will do to the community. I mean, we are all so trusting and accepting of each other and newcomers. That's bound to change."

"And the investigators have no idea who might be responsible?"

Ellie shook her head. "No, so far they have no evidence and not a clue. Not that they've admitted it," Ellie said. "What they do say is they cannot comment because of the ongoing investigations, which to Kirsten and me translates as they don't have a clue."

Ellie's cell phone rang. She pulled it from her purse, and glanced at the readout. Frowning, she answered the call.

"Hello?" Noticing Janelle's obvious curiosity, she continued, "Hi, Thomas. How is everything going with the reconstruction? Good. Ummmm, yes, I can meet you at my house in about an hour. What is this about? Okay, I can wait until then. See you then, goodbye."

Ellie clicked off her phone and took another sip of the cooling tea. "How odd. Thomas Wagner, the Maywood House administrator, is coming over to talk to me about something that is obviously serious. But he didn't want to discuss it on the phone. I wonder what's up. Do you suppose he has an idea who set fire to the home?

Janelle shrugged. "Possibly, but wouldn't he have called Kirsten or the police? It's more likely he has some information about the reconstruction he would like to get into the Courier."

"Yes, that makes sense. But why not just tell me?"

"Well, you'll find out soon enough," Janelle responded. "Give me a call afterward because now I'm really curious."

With a final warm hug and a paper plate of lemon bars, Ellie drove home and put on a pot of coffee. She uncovered the cookies and set them on the kitchen table. By the time the coffee had perked, Thomas was knocking at her front door.

As she led him to the living room and went to pour coffee, she was startled to see Oscar materialize into one of the easy chairs. Now she was truly puzzled. Settling into a chair across from Thomas, she set the tray of coffee mugs and cookies down on the coffee table. After a few moments of silence while they stirred and nibbled, Thomas began to speak.

"Ellie, you know we have about two months of work on the lesser damaged wing before Maywood House will be ready to receive residents again," he said. "I have a bit of a dilemma. You remember Maybelle Swain?" At Ellie's nod, he continued, "Well, she has been released from the hospital, of course, and has been staying with family. Now, her family tells me they just cannot continue to care for her. The adults both work and their teenaged kids are in school all day. They have asked if I can find a place for her to live until the wing is ready."

Ellie carefully set her coffee cup down and leaned back in the chair. "That sounds more as if they don't want the responsibility. And you are asking if I can take her in for a couple of months?"

Thomas sighed in relief. "You understand."

"Yes, of course I do, but Thomas, I work now. I'm afraid she would be alone here, too"

"I thought about that," he replied. "Maybelle is one of our assisted-living residents so she doesn't need skilled care so much as she needs some supervision to ensure she remembers to take her medications and eat properly. And surely, you have neighbors and friends who can drop in when you are going to be gone for a significant length of time to check on her?"

"Yes, I'm certain I do, but…"

Thomas leaned forward, anxiety etched on his face. "Ellie, Maybelle is one of my dearest resident friends. I cannot bear for her to suffer any more than she already has because of this ugly arson business. She spent days in the hospital, then moved in with a family that has no place or time for her. All she wants is to be at home in Creekwood, the only home she has known for 15 years. Add to that the fear and anguish this fire has caused not only Maybelle but all the other residents and the staff."

Ellie sat silent, while her thoughts swirled furiously. Question upon question presented itself.

"Okay, I need more information," she finally responded. "First, can she use the stairs? There's no bedroom on this floor. Does she need a special bed? What about the shower? And…"

Thomas held up a hand, stopping her. "We will provide anything she needs. She can go up and down stairs with assistance. She has a walker and cane when she wants to move around or go anywhere. If your beds don't work out for her, we will send over a hospital bed. We will install grab bars, a bath chair, and whatever else is needed in the bathroom. Several of our nursing staff members are still in the area and waiting to come back to work. I will ask them to come, on request, if you need them. In other words, I will do whatever it takes. I am heartsick about our residents. Many won't be coming back. They are already settled into other assisted living facilities. But Maybelle insists on returning to Maywood House and I personally will do all I can to make certain that happens for her."

Ellie took a few more minutes to consider his request.

"Okay, Thomas, this is what I want to do. I want to think this through very carefully. Then I will call a few friends to see how available they will be if needed. I promise to call you tomorrow morning with my decision. Is that okay with you?"

Thomas stood, leaned over the coffee table, and grasped Ellie's hand.

"Bless you for even considering this, Ellie," he gushed. "You are one of the kindest, most understanding people I know. Bless you for considering taking Maybelle in. I pray you will find it in your heart to open your home to her."

Ellie saw Thomas to the door and returned to the living room to pick up the coffee things. Oscar followed her into the kitchen where Angel was curled in her favorite place in front of the oven.

"Ellie, please."

Ellie silently rinsed the cups and covered the cookies before putting them in the refrigerator.

"Ellie, she will never, not for one moment, be alone."

Angel added her two-cents worth with a soft "mrrrreow."

Ellie gazed from Oscar's worried face to Angel's steady stare.

"Let me make some phone calls," she said.

Ellie called Janelle, who readily agreed to be on call if needed. Then Ellie put on a jacket and walked across the back yards to Catherine's home. Seated at the kitchen table, Ellie explained about Maybelle's dilemma. To her surprise, Catherine didn't hesitate to offer help as well.

"I can come over or you could bring her here for a visit," Catherine added. "I cannot imagine what it must be like, to lose your home like that and to be at loose ends at our age. But, it must be awful to feel your own family doesn't want you. That kind of rejection is more than miserable."

After a short visit, Ellie walked home. Shrugging out of her jacket, she went upstairs. The logical bedroom for Maybelle was Susan's old one, closest to the stairs and the bathroom. Stepping inside the rose and white little room, Ellie inspected it with a different eye, trying to see how Maybelle would manage. The bed was perhaps a bit low, which might make it hard for an older, somewhat disabled person to get up and down easily.

"Ellie, make a note," she quipped to herself. "Ask Thomas for something to help her stand up or raise the bed. Maybe we do need a hospital bed in here."

The closet and drawers were empty, so Maybelle would have plenty of space for her personal belongings. Ellie frowned, then mentally measured the doorway and the space around the bed. Would Maybelle be able to bring her walker into the room and still maneuver around? How were they going to get the walker up and down the stairs? Maybe she could borrow a second, narrower walker for upstairs. That might work.

Ellie checked out the bathroom with critical eyes. The toilet was close to the back wall. Would Maybelle need a booster seat? Was that going to cause problems when they installed grab bars? Was the tub too high for Maybelle to step into? How was she going to get in and out safely? Would she need help? Ellie sighed, then was struck by a horrific vision. This could easily be her in a few years. Now she was going to get a first-hand experience in how to prepare for her own elderly future. The thought sent her downstairs to the kitchen, where she pulled the remaining cookies out of the refrigerator and put the kettle on for tea.

"So, what do you say?"

Ellie turned around to see Oscar seated at the back corner of the kitchen table.

"I believe this could work," she cautiously answered. "I'm just afraid…"

"Ellie, I promise you, not only will Maybelle be perfectly at home here, but you will be blessed," Oscar pronounced.

"Okay, I am leaning toward saying yes," Ellie replied. "I'll call Thomas in the morning before I go to the editorial planning meeting."

Oscar was already fading away as he said, "I can't wait to tell Maybelle. She's going to be so very happy."

And then he was gone, leaving Ellie with lingering concerns about her sanity.

# CHAPTER 11

By the time Ellie arrived at the meeting Tuesday afternoon, Maybelle's move into her home was pretty much settled. The Courier's front page was dramatic, and at the same time sad. Most of the meeting involved follow-up articles and speculation about who could have done such a terrible thing as burn down a church. Ellie shared the information she had found online.

"We could be talking about someone who lives here but works out of town," Kirsten offered after a few moments' thought. "I mean, what if this person has, or had, a job that took him out of town a lot? What if, for some reason, he was fired, pardon the pun, or laid off? Now he is not only home all the time, prone to setting fires, but also he would be very angry."

Her words were greeted with a deep, uncomfortable silence. Finally Noel stirred.

"That's a lot of 'what ifs,' but you may be onto something," Noel said. "The question is how do we narrow down the possible suspects without drawing dangerous attention? We would need to be very subtle."

"Why don't we tell the police what we think?" Ellie asked. "I mean, they are the ones conducting the investigation."

Kirsten turned to Ellie. "Police investigate facts and evidence. We have neither, just hunches. They may listen but they'll be skeptical. They would pat us on our backs, thank us for our concern, and firmly suggest we leave the crime solving to the experts."

Noel nodded. "Kirsten is right," he agreed. "They'll probably just blow us off. No, we need to do our own investigative reporting but at the same time be extremely circumspect about how we do it and to whom we talk. Ellie, you are in the best position to help. Think about the people you know and make a list of anyone who might fit Kirsten's description. But, don't go asking questions on your own. It's too dangerous."

The rest of the editorial meeting went on as usual with assignments handed out. When the business part of the meeting wrapped up, Noel said, "I have an announcement to make. AP has picked up your stories and photos on the lodge fire. That means they will be shared with other newspapers across the country. Good job, ladies, and Jason.'

After high-fives around, Noel continued, "Ellie, I want to see you in my office for a moment, please."

Ignoring the knowing looks and raised eyebrows, Ellie logged off her computer, put her jacket on, and reluctantly went to Noel's office. He shut the door behind her.

"Ellie, have you given any thought to what I said about having someone stay with you until they catch this arsonist?"

Ellie sighed. Knowing Noel wasn't going to like it, she responded, "I am going to have someone staying with me for at least the next two months."

Noel waited, leaning back in his chair, arms crossed through a long silence. "And?"

Ellie took a deep breath. "Thomas Anderson has asked me to take in Maybelle Swain until the Maywood House's new wing is completed."

Noel's chair crashed down as he lunged upward, his hands landing on the desk with a force that shook the metal desk. "What? That is not what I meant when I suggested you find someone to protect you," he roared. "Are you out of your mind? That woman will be more of a handicap than help. That means the arsonist has two targets in one place."

Ellie rose from her chair and leaned over the desk until she and Noel were nearly nose to nose. "And exactly what business is it of yours?" she stated. "I am an adult. I am capable of taking care of myself. I am hardly a target, as you suggest. In fact, that's pretty far-fetched, Noel. And besides, I have help."

Ellie stopped short. She could hardly explain Oscar to Noel. The big-city editor would snort and comment sarcastically that she was more in need of assistance than even she knew.

"If you want me to continue working for the Courier, I respectfully ask you to keep this relationship businesslike," Ellie concluded. She picked up her purse and left Noel's office without a backward look. In the reception area, Martha sat with her eyes wide and her mouth hanging open as Ellie strode past her desk, and out the front door.

Noel rounded his desk and stood in the office doorway. He leaned against the doorframe with his arms crossed and glared out the windows, watching as Ellie got into her car and carefully backed out of the parking slot. He sighed deeply, a mixture of anger and worry at war on his face. Then he glanced over at Martha, turned, and re-entered his office, closing the door firmly behind him.

Ellie's hands shook on the steering wheel as she slowly drove up Main. Taking several deep breaths, she tried to push the anger and confusion away and focus on what she needed to do before Maybelle moved in on Friday. She was passing the Atrium when she had a sudden, strong urge to stop and see if the bakery had any of those coconut pecan scones left. Buying something she loved to eat would ease the agitation she was feeling. Besides, those scones with their crowns of rich chocolate glaze were enough to make any kind of situation seem better.

Inside the Atrium, Ellie saw the owner's teen daughter behind the bakery counter, a cheery red apron wrapped around her slender frame. Ellie nodded to her and continued to study the trays piled with cookies, scones, cupcakes, and tarts that lined the glassed-in display cases.

"Can I help you, Mrs. Franklyn?"

Ellie smiled at her over the counter and glanced at her name tag. "Yes, Jenny. I would like two of those pecan coconut scones, one of the peach cupcakes and two of the walnut brownies."

While the teen boxed up her order, Ellie wandered around the light, cheery space lined with specialty foods on lacy white metal shelves between the windows. Just the aroma of baking was enough to sooth Ellie's ragged nerves. She turned as Jenny asked, "Will that be all?"

Ellie chose a box of English breakfast tea from one of the shelves and returned to the cashier station. "This should do it," she said with a grin.

Jenny smiled back. "Well, if it doesn't, you can always come back. Mom has a batch of triple chocolate cupcakes cooling and nearly ready to be frosted."

"Mercy," Ellie joked back. "Thanks for the temptation!"

Ellie drove home with the scent of sweet treats and a more relaxed feeling. In the kitchen, she put the kettle on for tea and put one of the scones on a small plate. Angel rose from her place by the oven and curled around Ellie's legs, purring softly. Ellie pulled the receipt from the box, closed it, and pushed it to the back of the counter. She was about to crumple the receipt and throw it in the garbage when she noticed writing on the back.

Again, it was a telephone number. Ellie had completely forgotten about the one on her luncheon receipt. Now she compared the two and saw they were the same. No question who wrote it _ Jenny Olmstead. And hadn't she suspected the teen girl wanted her attention for some reason when she had brunch at the Atrium Sunday? Ellie didn't hesitate this time. Ellie dialed the number and when Jenny answered, she was surprised at the tremor of fear in her voice.

"Mrs. Franklin? I need to talk to you but it can't be here or anywhere we can be seen," Jenny whispered. "I think I know who the arsonist is."

Ellie gasped. "Wouldn't it be safer just to talk on the phone?"

"No, I can't be certain no one is listening," Jenny responded. "I have school tomorrow. If I walk over to Founder's park and just stroll along, you could do the same and we could sort of run into each other near the gazebo. Would that work?"

Ellie agreed it could. "It would have to look accidental, so timing is important. What time do you get out of school?"

Jenny replied, "About 2:45 and it would take around 10 minutes to walk into the park."

Ellie thought for a moment. "Okay, how about if I park at the far end in the river lot and take my camera. I can be taking photos of the river and just run into you. Does that sound right?"

Jenny said, "Yes, that should be okay. You can pretend you are showing me your camera."

"Good, I'll see you tomorrow around 3 p.m., and Jenny... be careful."

Ellie hung up and immediately called Kirsten.

"Kirsten, the reason I'm calling is someone reached out to me this afternoon," Ellie told her colleague. "I'm to meet this person at 3 p.m. in Founders' Park. I am not afraid of this person, but I am a bit concerned about going alone. And, what if the information is correct, and someone is stalking him or her?"

Kirsten was silent for a moment. "My advice is go, but act causal. Make it look as if you happened to take a walk in the park and bumped into this person by accident. Keep your voices low to avoid being overheard. Actually, the playground is a good choice. The area around it is open, good visibility. Just sit where you can watch the wooded area along the river. And have your informant sit watching the street and parking lot."

Ellie almost laughed out loud. "My goodness, you make this sound like a spy movie," she exclaimed. "Truth is, that's pretty much what I was thinking but not so much about the playground. We could bump into each other there."

"Take it seriously, Ellie. You may be dealing with a witness who can help pinpoint a killer. Be careful."

Ellie said she would, then added, "And whatever you do, don't tell Noel."

Kirsten laughed. "Yeah, I hear you. In fact, the entire building heard Noel this afternoon."

"Oh, my goodness," Ellie groaned. "How embarrassing. What am I going to do?"

"Probably nothing is the best choice," Kirsten replied. "Face it, Noel is smitten, has been since he first saw you."

Ellie sighed. "Well, I hope he gets over it. I am nowhere ready for any kind of romantic relationship. It's been barely three months since I lost Jerry."

"Yes, but Noel doesn't fully appreciate that," Kirsten said. "He wasn't here, he didn't know Jerry, and besides remember what I said about feelings? Be patient. This will resolve itself one way or another. Meanwhile, be safe and call me when you get home."

Ellie ended the call, poured water into a mug, and dropped one of the new teabags into it. She carried the mug and plate to the table and sat down just as Oscar popped in. She was getting so used to having the spirit appear that she didn't even react.

"I heard," Oscar said. "You won't be going to the park alone tomorrow, Ellie. I will be there with you. I can make sure no one is close by."

"Thank you," Ellie replied. After blowing on her tea to cool it, she thought for a minute, and then asked, "Oscar, what can you do if we run into trouble?"

Oscar frowned. "I am not really sure."

Ellie set the mug down and stared across the table at Oscar. "What do you mean, you aren't sure?"

Oscar shook his head. "I don't always know what I am allowed to do and to what extent. When I helped those firefighters escape, I just did what anyone would have done. But there appears to be subtle differences between what a live person can do and what a spirit is allowed to do."

"What you are saying is that you are not allowed to interfere if something is meant to be, right?" Ellie said. "I don't know if that is good or bad, under the circumstances."

"Right, but whatever happens, I will be there for you, Ellie. I'll scout around and, if there is someone lurking around, you will see me."

And Ellie supposed that having Oscar watch her back was as good as it was going to get.

The dashboard clock read 2:50 when Ellie parked her car at the far end of Founders' Park. Dressed in warm clothing with her camera case slung over one shoulder, she felt as if she was starring in a thriller movie. Shaking her head ruefully, she locked the car and flipped the hood up over her head. The afternoon was chill and damp. An impish breeze poked rude fingers up her sleeves and down the sides of the hood. Ellie began walking along the recreational pathway that followed the riverbank through the park. She kept reminding herself that she was just going for a walk like any other Creekwood resident might do. Meeting up with Jenny had to look incidental, casual, just in case someone was watching.

Nevertheless, she was startled to see the teen sitting on top of a picnic bench next to the swings. Jenny waved and Ellie strolled across the ground. Raising a finger to her lips, Ellie said softly, "Whisper. Sound carries here."

Jenny nodded. The two sat side-by-side on the table. Ellie pulled her camera out of its case and showed Jenny a few of its functions. Ellie finally turned more toward Jenny so she could see both the wooded riverbank and a good portion of the parallel roadway.

"What do you want to tell me," she prompted.

Jenny took a deep breath. "I'm scared. My best friend Amy is dating Gerald Brady, a senior at Creekwood High. Both of us believe that Gerald's father is the arsonist."

Ellie studies the teen's face beneath her jacket hood. "Why do you and Amy think he's the one?"

"Well, Gerald said his dad was fired from his sales job a couple of months ago," Jenny began. "Since then, Mr. Brady has been depressed, really moody and gets angry for no reason at all. He hit Gerald's mom a couple of times, and that's totally not the way he used to be."

Ellie nodded encouragingly. "Go on."

"Amy and I started checking. Mr. Brady wasn't home every single night there was a fire," Jenny continued. "After the Maywood House fire, he came home smelling of smoke and gas. Amy was at Gerald's house, doing homework and she told me. When the lodge caught fire, I snuck out and tried to see if Mr. Brady was anywhere near the fire. That's when you saw me. Boy, did you scare me!"

Ellie chuckled softly. "You scared me, too. But Jenny, what do you want me to do about this? The police won't investigate unless they have some kind of solid proof against Mr. Brady."

Jenny sighed. "Then you believe me? Oh, thank you! I ... er, Amy and I were hoping you would investigate it at the newspaper. That way, if you find out anything, you can share it with the police. Amy and I won't be mentioned, will we? Aren't we what they call 'confidential sources.' Boy, that sounds weird even to me."

Ellie thought for a moment. "I will never divulge a source. I can talk to Kirsten Patrick and the editor, Noel Hathaway, about what my source passed on. Do you know who Mr. Brady worked for? If we know, we can track where he has been, and see if there were other arson incidents that match his travel schedule."

Jenny nodded. "He used to work for Smithfield Engineering and, before that, for a company that sold elevators and maintenance services. Amy told me he traveled a lot, mostly around the Midwest like Illinois,

Indiana, Michigan, maybe Iowa. And Wisconsin, naturally."

Ellie was about to reply when Oscar abruptly appeared. She gasped softly, then murmured to Jenny, "Someone is close by and we need to end this conversation. You can email me at the newspaper office... efranklyn@cc.com. Now, which way did you come from."

Jenny had jumped to her feet. She whispered, "The street."

"Pretend you're answering your cell. Go back the way you came. I am going to continue my walk so it doesn't look so much like we met deliberately."

"But Mrs. Franklyn, if it's Mr. Brady, he's dangerous. Shouldn't you go back to your car?"

"No, it's going to be okay. Now go on, Jenny. Stay in close touch."

Ellie eased down from the picnic table and walked away from Jenny, away from where her car was parked. She saw Jenny dash off toward home and felt Oscar's comforting presence at her side.

"Ellie," he began.

Ellie glanced sideways, then whispered, "Where is he? Just keep an eye on him. I need to protect Jenny. She's doing the right thing, and I don't want anything to happen to her because of it. Besides, I feel safe with you guarding me."

The next 10 minutes were tense. Ellie pretended to take photos of the park, river, and playground while she halfway expected to be confronted by Mr. Brady. But the park remained still and seemingly empty. Finally, she stopped and looked down at her wristwatch. Shrugging her jacket closer, Ellie didn't have to pretend to be cold. She turned and retraced her steps back along the rec path, she could feel the hair stir on the back of her neck and a vague itching at the center of her back.

"He's still there, isn't he?"

"I believe he is," Oscar confirmed. "Let's hope he bought the act. It was a pretty good one, actually."

Ellie nearly laughed out loud. "I hope so. I barely know Jenny. That should work in our favor. Or maybe not. I don't know how people like this arsonist think. But Oscar, did you see who it was?"

"I did, but I don't know who he is or why he's where he is," Oscar replied. At Ellie's perplexed expression, Oscar continued, "Ellie, I am a spirit but I'm not Superman. It was a fairly good-sized man lurking in the shadows of the trees."

Back at the parking lot, Ellie quickly got into her car and locked the doors. She started it up, then pulled her cell from the purse she had left behind. Drat, I'm not so good as this as I think. I should have had the phone in my pocket.

As the car warmed, she started to call Kirsten, then stopped and put the cell down. It would look to an outsider as if she were reporting on a meeting. She decided it would be best to wait until she was home and not under the potential eye of a killer.

With the teapot heating and the peach cupcake perched on a napkin, Ellie dialed Kirsten's number. The call went straight to message mode.

"Hi. I think we need to meet in Noel's office tomorrow morning first thing," Ellie reported. "You were definitely on to something. I just learned that one of Creekwood's residents fits the profile you talked about. See you tomorrow."

# CHAPTER 12

When Ellie parked in front of the Creekwood Courier, she could see Noel and Kirsten already seated in his office through the plate glass window. She walked in past Martha, put her jacket and purse on her desk, then straightened her shoulders and went back past Martha to the office door.

"Come in, Ellie, and please close the door behind you."

Noel's voice was flat but his expression was grim. Ellie could literally feel the control he was using. Kirsten wasn't smiling, either. Both waited until Ellie settled into the other chair. Then Noel leaned forward with his arms on the desk.

"Okay, Ellie. Kirsten says you called this meeting after talking to a source yesterday," Noel began. "Why don't you start at the beginning and tell us what you've learned."

Ellie registered not only the barely controlled anger but also restraint with which Noel spoke. What Noel didn't say spoke volumes. She composed herself and went over the events again in her mind.

"Someone reached out to me yesterday after the editorial meeting," Ellie said. "We met yesterday afternoon in the park. The source told me that a friend's father might be the arsonist."

"What did this person base this supposition on?" Kirsten asked, leaning forward as well.

"The suspect recently lost his job. Since then, he has been depressed, prone to unreasoning anger and hit his wife on two occasions," Ellie began. "After the Maywood House fire, he came home smelling of smoke and gasoline. He was not at home on every night that fires were set. The source is frightened, as are friends close to the suspect."

"Did this source name the suspect?"

Ellie sighed. "Yes. His name is Matthew Brady. He worked as a traveling consultant for an engineering company until late January. Everything I was told fits with what little we know. It seems, Kirsten, as if your instincts were right on the money."

Noel leaned back and gazed off for a moment. "So, how do we want to handle this? Do we take this info to the police or start our own investigation, or both."

"Well, as we said before, the police will want proof and we don't have anything solid," Kirsten mused. "We can start a search online to see where suspected arsons in other cities match up with the engineering company's clients but without knowing Mr. Brady's schedule, I don't see how that will help us."

Noel nodded. "I agree. That would be a very long shot."

"Maybe, if Kirsten begins asking leading questions at the police department, they might be led to focus their investigation," Ellie said tentatively. "I mean, instead of just telling them we suspect Mr. Brady, Kirsten could ask if they had looked at potential suspects using the same criteria she did with her profile."

Kirsten smiled for the first time. "That might work. Even if they think I'm crazy, someone over there just might buy into the idea. I can plant those hints when I go over to update the investigation this afternoon. All I really need do is ask the right questions."

Noel made some notes on a reporter's tablet, then looked up abruptly at Ellie. "Anything else you want to tell us?"

Ellie hesitated and that said it all.

"What?"

Ellie took a deep breath. "While I was talking to the source, someone was there in the park watching us."

The silence that greeted her words was deadly.

"And you know this how?" Noel muttered between clenched teeth.

How do I explain this one, Ellie wondered. "Ummm, I had this very uncomfortable feeling…"

Noel slammed his fist down on the desk.

"Noel," Kirsten said softly. "Easy does it."

But Noel wasn't listening. "Just a feeling, Ellie, or do you know for a fact there was someone there?"

When in doubt, go with the truth, Ellie reminded herself of her mother's adage.

"Someone was there," she simply stated.

Noel and Kirsten gazed at each other, then Kirsten shook her head. She slipped out of her chair and left the office, closing the door gently behind her.

Noel glared at Ellie, who refused to be intimidated by his anger. Or was it anger, she asked herself. Maybe what she was reading in his eyes was concern or fear. Or, she added, an exaggerated sense of responsibility for an employee. Trouble was, Ellie was worried as well, not only for herself but also for Jenny, and Amy and Gerald, too. She realized that she shouldn't underestimate the danger they were in now. After all, the arsonist had killed a child, even if it was what they callously call "collateral damage." He wouldn't stop at killing again. And, if Jenny's information was correct, Mr. Brady was unraveling at a frightening speed.

"Yelling at you obviously doesn't work," Noel finally said. "I don't know what to say or do to keep you safe."

"You don't need to keep me safe, as you say," Ellie responded. "I am not your responsibility."

Noel shook his head ruefully. "Yes, you are, whether or not you want to accept it. Ellie, I have strong feelings for you. I understand that on several levels, they may be deemed inappropriate not only by you but also by the community. But I am not going to deny what I feel. I care deeply about you. I have from the moment I saw you. I don't understand why, but I felt the connection and, I think, so do you. So the question now is, what do we do about it?"

Ellie nearly panicked. But then she remembered her mother's adage once again. "I'm not ready to do anything about it," she murmured. Having said that, Ellie realized she had acknowledged both Noel's feelings and, inadvertently, her own. "I'm just not ready," she repeated softly, then stood and left the office. Behind her, she heard Noel grunt. Whether it was in disappointment or some other emotion, she couldn't say.

Back at her desk, Ellie resolutely began sorting PSAs into chronological order. Across the desk, she felt rather than saw Kirsten's intense study. Then Kirsten chuckled.

"You know, when I came here, I was afraid I was going to be bored with a small town's notion of news," Kirsten said. "I planned on getting a year or so in experience before moving on to a bigger market. But now, it's like watching a soap opera around here. I can't wait to see what happens next."

Ellie snorted. "Glad I'm so entertaining!"

Kirsten laughed out loud. "Oh, it's not so much your relationship with Noel. It's everything! All the wicked little politics, rumors, gossip, and even the everyday life of a small town. The arson is just the frosting on a very rich, addictive cake. I mean, who needs, drugs, gangs and drive-by shootings? In bigger cities, reports get the news but not necessarily the nuance. Creekwood is Chicago under a microscope. The view may be narrowed but that doesn't seem to lessen the content."

Ellie grumbled, "Well, you're really cheerful today. If I didn't know better, I might think you were in love."

Kirsten stopped laughing. Ellie glanced across the desk and was taken aback at the astonished look on Kirsten's face. But, before either one could say anything, Noel rushed into the editorial area and leaned close to Ellie.

"Did you mention ... ah, what we suspect... to anyone else?" he whispered.

Ellie realized he didn't want Martha to overhear. "No, just the two of you," she murmured. "Since I don't know Mr. ... ah, the suspect... it would seem strange for me to ask about him."

Noel nodded. "Good thinking," he said, obviously relieved. "Let's keep it that way. Ellie, please don't say anything to anyone. And Kirsten, be very careful who you talk to about this. I am seriously concerned for your safety as well."

After Noel went back to his office, Ellie gazed meaningfully across at Kirsten, then quirked one eyebrow. Kirsten actually blushed.

"Ummmm, later," she said softly with a nod toward the reception area.

"I'll hold you to that," Ellie replied. Glancing at her watch, she added, "I need to be at the Methodist Church for an advance on their upcoming children's Easter egg hunt. They are starting to stuff plastic eggs with candies this morning. I expect Jason to meet me there. Talk to you later."

Ellie stopped by Martha's desk to let her know where she would be, then drove over to the church. About a dozen cars were parked close to the side door. Jason was waiting by his car, hunched over in a heavy jacket and loaded down with photography gear.

"Is this winter ever going to end?" he grouched. "I just heard on the radio that we might get snow flurries that Saturday, just in time to ruin the kids' egg hunt."

Ellie nodded. "I heard that, too. Thanks for mentioning it. I can ask what their alternative plans are, in case the weather is too lousy."

Together they walked into the church and followed the sound of laughter downstairs to the kitchen area. About 20 women and men were seated around tables piled with bags of pastel plastic eggs and wrapped candies. Jason immediately began taking closeup pictures while Ellie pulled a chair close to the hunt chairperson.

Hi, Ellie!" Mavis Crocker said. "Go pour yourself a cup of coffee and grab a couple of these cookies," she added, pushing a large platter of dainty sugar cookies within Ellie's reach.

"I'll get it," someone headed toward the kitchen called out.

"Thanks, I need it," Ellie called back. "Boy, it's chilly out there, not what we normally expect for April. Yeah, I know… it's very early April."

"April? In Wisconsin?" Mavis replied with a chuckle. "We could still get snow."

Ellie nodded, pulling out her notepad. "Don't I know it? So, what happens if the weather is too cold or wet?"

Mavis shrugged. "I guess we stash eggs all over the sanctuary. It's the biggest space inside. We still haven't figured out how to separate the older children's hunt from the younger ones if it comes to that. Maybe one up and one down? I think we are all praying we don't have to figure it out."

Ellie asked several more questions about the popular event that attracted more than 100 children from all over the area. Meanwhile, Jason wandered around the tables, nibbling on cookies and taking shots. He followed one of the volunteers into the kitchen and did a couple more shots of him filling coffee mugs, a plate of cookies on the counter beside him. With the story notes and photos nailed, Ellie and Jason headed back to the office.

Ellie was deep into writing the advance when Jason abruptly appeared beside her desk. He was frowning at his camera screen.

"Ellie, look at this pic," he said, passing the camera over to her. "I did this medium-range shot of the guy in the kitchen from just outside the doorway. But, this is weird. Look at the window above the sink."

Ellie stared into the camera screen. High above the volunteer's head, a narrow horizontal window allowed daylight to fall into the basement kitchen. A shadowy person was crouched down close to the glass, his face peering intently into the church's kitchen. Trouble was, he was just outside the camera's focal point. While it was definitely a man in dark clothing, it was next to impossible to determine who he was.

Ellie gasped. "We need to show this to Noel immediately," she exclaimed.

She jumped up from her desk and led a puzzled Jason into Noel's office without even knocking. Since Martha was out to lunch, she didn't close the door. Noel looked up at them with an impatient grimace. But, when he saw the expression on Ellie's face, his changed to concern.

"What?" he demanded.

"You need to see this photo Jason took at the Methodist Church," Ellie answered, handing the camera over to him. "See, in the window above the man?"

Noel nodded grimly. "Someone was watching you," he stated flatly. "I was afraid of this."

Jason looked totally befuddled. It was his turn to ask, "What?"

"Sit down Jason, Ellie," Noel directed. "We need to get you up to speed, especially since you may have just joined the list of the endangered."

While Noel outlined their suspicions about the serial arsonist being Matthew Brady, Ellie listened but her mind was on something else entirely. Maybelle Swain was moving into her home in two days. Her children would all be arriving to spend Easter weekend with her, just 10 days from now. The timing couldn't possibly be worse, she mused. Her attention returned to Noel and Jason as they were going over the photos before and after the one with the watcher.

"He must have seen me step into the kitchen," Jason was saying. "I only caught him on camera once."

Noel studied the photo more closely. "Hmmm, is there any way to make the image clearer?"

Jason sighed. "It's not like CSI, boss. We don't have programs that can reassemble pixels, and neither does the Creekwood PD."

"Jason? Didn't you take photos of the onlookers at all the fires?" Ellie asked.

Jason brightened. "Wow, that's right! I have them all archived on the network. But, do you know what Matthew Brady looks like? I don't know him at all, and I don't remember ever taking a photo of him."

Noel and Ellie both shook their heads.

"We need to get a candid shot of Brady for comparison. I'll volunteer for that," Noel decided. "I can figure out a way to find him and use my phone. That way we will at least put a face to the stalker."

At Ellie's muffled grunt, Noel said lightly, "Hey, just add me to the endangered species list. If he catches me at it, that is. Besides, the more people Brady thinks he has to watch, the better. I mean, he cannot possibly keep track of all of us, right? And maybe one or more of us can start watching him."

As Ellie and Jason returned to their desks, Kirsten breezed in.

"Okay! I believe I have successfully planted the seeds of suspicion at the PD," she declared. "Ahhh, the joys of artful rediretion… what?"

"You need to see the photo Jason shot at the church this morning," Ellie told her.

Kirsten set her purse and notepad down on her desk, then walked back to where Jason was downloading photos onto his computer. All was quiet until the moment Kirsten saw the telltale photo. Ellie heard her gasp, then exclaim, "Oh, my god!"

"Yup," Jason replied. "I have officially joined the ranks of the stalked. You are probably included, too, Kirsten. Guilt by association."

Kirsten returned to her desk and plopped down in the chair. "Wow, that means you and Jason and your source are all being stalked."

Ellie smiled grimly. "Yes, and Noel, too. He's going to try to secretly photo Brady because none of us knows what he looks like. Jason can scan the crowd pics from the fires to see if he's there."

"More fuel for the fire, if you'll pardon the pun," Kirsten quipped. "This just might all work in our favor. You know that old saying, 'divide and conquer?' What we can do is a reverse on it, divide up and keep him busy until we have solid proof he's the arsonist."

Ellie shook her head. "But there's nothing to keep him from picking us off one by one," she pointed out. "And I'm very concerned about my source."

"Why?"

"Too close and too vulnerable," Ellie said. "Plus, I have Maybelle moving in Friday and my whole family coming for Easter in little more than a week."

Kirsten nodded. "Look, if you feel you need someone there, I can move in temporarily, just for the week until your family arrives."

"Thanks, Kirsten, I'll seriously consider that."

As Kirsten turned to her computer and opened her notepad, Ellie tried to focus on the PSAs. At the back of her mind, she wondered how much help Oscar would be if

Brady came after her or Maybelle. He hadn't been able to reassure her that he could or would intercede. Oscar may have rescued the firefighters at the lodge but what if, when the moment came, he was constrained from interfering? What then? Was she still on her own with the unwanted attention of a killer?

# CHAPTER 13

By Sunday night, any fears that Ellie may have harbored about having Maybelle as a housemate were gone. Maybelle proved to be a lot more spry than Ellie expected an eighty-something person to be. And it was funny to watch Oscar dote on the witty little lady with the twinkling blue eyes. They are really sort of in love, Ellie thought with dazed amazement as she loaded laundry in the dryer.

She came upstairs to find them in the kitchen, arranging snickerdoodles on a plate and heating water for tea. Ellie just had to smile. They looked like an old married couple, not simply an old lady and an old ghost. She sank down onto a chair and shook her head, still smiling.

"You two look as if you have been together for decades," Ellie finally said.

Oscar turned with a startled expression on his usually deadpan face. "Why, we have, Ellie," he replied. "Maybelle was the first resident I became acquainted with when my house was converted into a retirement home."

Maybelle laughed. "And I remember the first night we met, so to speak. I was getting ready for bed when Oscar just sort of popped into the room. I was, well, not fully clothed at the time. I'm not sure which one of us was more embarrassed."

Ellie gasped. "My goodness, Oscar! You didn't know she wasn't dressed?"

"My dear Ellie," he said pompously, "I can walk through walls but I can't see through them. Besides, I didn't think she would see me. No one else had, not Thomas nor the staff nor the renovation crew. It came as quite a shock, let me tell you."

A soft knock on the kitchen door drew their attention. Frowning, Ellie answered the door to find Kirsten and a young man Ellie recognized as one of Creekwood's firefighters, though he was out of uniform.

Ellie invited them inside. Maybelle piled a dozen more cookies on the plate and carried it into the living room while Ellie pulled more mugs from the cupboard and poured hot water into the teapot. She dropped in four Earl Grey teabags into the pot and loaded it along with the mugs, cream, sugar and lemon wedges onto a tray. Oscar trailed along behind. It was obvious neither Kirsten nor the firefighter could see him.

Kirsten settled on the sofa. The young man sat close beside her. Maybelle chose a side chair and set the cookie plate on the coffee table, pushing it in front of the two visitors. Ellie set the tea tray down beside the cookies and sat in the other side chair. Oscar leaned against the fireplace mantle, a perplexed expression on his face. For several minutes, everyone busied themselves pouring and picking up cookies. Then the room became uncomfortably quiet.

"Okay," Kirsten finally blurted. "I guess I had better come clean here. This is Joe Walters. I know you recognize him as a fireman, Ellie. Joe and I have been, well, seeing each other for a while."

Oscar's left eyebrow shot up. Ellie stared at the couple as the implications of what Kirsten said sunk in. In the silence, Maybelle smiled brightly.

"Why, that is simply delightful," she chirped, beaming at the two young people.

"Yes, delightful," Ellie echoed.

Maybelle turned to gaze at Ellie. "What's the matter, dear?" she softly whispered.

"Kirsten is our hard news reporter. Joe is a firefighter. They're not supposed to be…ummmm," Ellie began glumly.

"But of course," Maybelle replied. "That must make for awkward situations because of all the fire investigations."

Kirsten turned toward Maybelle eagerly. "Yes, I'm after information that Joe is not allowed to tell me. If I use what he does tell me, it will quickly become obvious that he is the source. I mean, the fire department isn't that big, and we have been seen together."

"Joe will possibly be suspended or fired, and you will destroy your working relationship with the department," Ellie pointed out even though it wasn't necessary to say it.

"The trouble is," Kirsten said earnestly, "we both know information we cannot use in the paper or at the department without exposing our relationship. It hasn't been a problem until the fires started. Now, we don't know what to do."

"So we were kind of hoping you would help us get the information out as a sort of decoy," Joe added. "You know everyone in town. We can …"

A sharp rap on the front door startled them into silence again.

"Now what?" Ellie muttered as she rose to answer the door. "No one who knows me uses the front door. I can't imagine who this could be."

Ellie flipped the switch for the front porch light and opened the door wide to find Noel Hathaway standing there with his fist out, ready to knock again.

"Oh!" Ellie exclaimed.

"Oh, oh," Kirsten murmured behind her.

"Oh, my!" Maybelle stated.

Oscar's other eyebrow shot up.

"May I come in?" Noel asked, peering past Ellie at the rest of the tea party.

"Ummm, yes, of course," Ellie replied, stepping aside so he could pass her. "I'll just fetch another mug."

While Ellie rushed into the kitchen, Noel took off his jacket and stared at Kirsten. Ellie came back in time to hear Noel say, "You are out of uniform, Firefighter Walters."

"This isn't an official visit," Joe responded, squirming a little.

"I am certain it's not," Noel answered grimly. "And this must be Miss Maybelle Swain. I'm pleased to meet you at last."

"And I am pleased to finally meet you, Mr. Hathaway," Maybelle grinned up at him. "Now, I know why all the ladies in town simper when your name is mentioned."

Despite the tension in the room, Noel laughed. Then he turned toward the fireplace and asked, "And who is this gentleman?"

Kirsten and Joe looked from Noel to the fireplace, clearly puzzled. Maybelle's face lit up with joy. Ellie's jaw dropped and she gasped, nearly dropping the mug in her hand. But Oscar was totally flummoxed.

"You can see him?" Ellie burst out.

"Of course I can see him," Noel snorted. "He's as plain as the nose on your face."

"Well then, let me introduce you," Ellie replied. "Noel, this is Oscar Maywood."

While Kirsten and Joe looked at each other in bewilderment, Noel very slowly turned his head until he met Oscar's gaze.

"Oscaar Maywood?" Noel muttered. "Isn't he… ummm… dead?"

Oscar grinned. "More or less, depending on your point of view," he quipped.

Ellie opened her mouth to try and explain, but before she could say a word, Joe stood and stepped carefully across the room to the fireplace. He waved his hand in front of him as if reaching out for a handhold. Then he turned around and frowned at Noel, a perplexed expression on his face.

"Are you saying that there's a man standing here that I can't see?" he exclaimed.

Kirsten looked from Ellie to Noel to Maybelle. "Wait a minute. You three can see him, but Joe and I can't, right? What is going on?"

Ellie sighed. "Kirsten, remember when I told you I had a source. I couldn't tell you who because I was fairly certain you wouldn't believe me. But look on the bright side, we can't get him in trouble."

Oscar laughed.

"And there's another thing you don't know," Maybelle chimed in. "Oscar is the hero of the lodge fire. He was in the fire and pulled those firefighters out before the entire building fell on them."

Joe looked stunned. "You mean, when Phil seemed to fly out of the way of that falling timber? That was … Oscar?"

Yes, it was," Ellie confirmed. "Oscar dragged the men close to the opening in the front and when only two of them were being pulled outside, he gave Phil a strong shove to get him away from the fire. I saw him in the flames."

Everyone stood silent, remembering that awful scene, except Maybelle, who was beaming and nodding.

Abruptly, Ellie took a deep breath and said, "I'll make more tea and bring some more cookies. Since we are all here, we may as well start working together on what we know, and what we can do to help stop Brady."

Kirsten stood up and followed Ellie into the kitchen. "I've heard of unimpeachable sources but, really, Ellie," she said with a rueful shake of her head. "This beats all. Is Oscar Maywood really standing in the living room?"

"Mrrrrrrrowww."

Kirsten gasped and jumped, then looked sheepish as Angel rose and stretched nonchalantly from her place on the rug in front of the oven.

"Oh, Angel sees him, too," Ellie replied with a grin.

Kirsten gazed at the little cat and grunted. "That's the cat from Maywood House, the one everyone said sounded the alarm when the fire broke out there, right?"

Ellie nodded. She picked up the kettle to fill it, then frowned. It looked as if it were going to be a long night. Resolutely, she set the kettle back on the stove and started making coffee. Kirsten's eyebrows went up, then she went back to the living room to see how the others felt about an impromptu meeting.

By the time the coffee was brewed, they were deeply embroiled into putting together facts to present to the police department. Ellie started a pro-and-con list while the others threw out ideas and facts. Ellie filled mugs and brought more cookies from the freezer that she had quickly thawed in the microwave.

Two hours passed, then three. As they gathered everything they had learned about the arsons and began to put them in logical, consecutive order, it became more and more clear that they were dealing with a deadly serial arsonist. They were close to wrapping up the meeting when suddenly, Joe's pager went off, warning him of an active fire and calling him to duty. At the same time, Noel's cell phone pinged.

As Joe rose to leave, Noel shouted into his phone, "What? Jason, are you okay? We're on our way right now."

Oscar had already vanished. Ellie ran to get a coat while the rest pulled theirs on. As they did, Noel filled them in on Jason's call.

"Jason was working at the office when he heard noises behind the building. He went to investigate and was just in time to see someone throw gasoline in the garbage bins and set them on fire," he ranted.

"Dear God, is he okay?" Maybelle breathed.

"Yes, he ducked back into the building and called 911. The police and fire are on their way now."

Ellie frowned. "But was Jason the target or just the building?"

"It doesn't matter," Kirsten declared. "Someone, I'm guessing Brady, just fired the first shot."

"Exactly," Noel replied. "Ellie, grab those notes and ride with me. Kirsten go with Joe. No one goes anywhere alone again until this is settled."

"But we're leaving Maybelle here alone," Ellie pointed out.

Noel grimaced. "Can you call someone?"

"I can call Catherine, my next door neighbor," she suggested. "It's late but I'm guessing she's still up."

Quickly Ellie made arrangements for Catherine to come over and keep Maybelle company, then joined Noel in his car. By this time, he was beyond impatient, drumming his fingers on the steering wheel, and muttering under his breath.

"Jason is okay, right?"

"Right."

"They caught the fire before it could do much damage to the office, right?"

"Right."

Ellie paused, then decided to go for it. "Then we have nothing to worry about with them. What we do need to do is be prepared because the police and fire chiefs are going to be asking a lot of tough questions."

# CHAPTER 14

As Noel's car sped through the darkened, quiet streets, Ellie sat in tense silence. Her thoughts were jumbled, flitting from wondering how much damage the fire had done to how they would get the paper out, and if Jason was uninjured. Noel tried to park behind the building as usual, before realizing that it was where the fire started. The area was blocked off. He quickly turned the car away from the area and found a space a block away down a Creekwood side street. Together, they exited the car and ran toward the front of the building.

"There's Kirsten and Joe," Noel panted. "I don't see Jason."

They skidded to a halt beside the other couple and turned to stare at the newspaper office. The front of the Creekwood Courier was brick façade while the side and rear walls were wooden siding. Old wooden siding, Ellie remembered, which meant it would probably burn rapidly. Acrid smoke filled the air, making it uncomfortable to breath but there was no sign of an active fire. Uniformed fire and police rushed back and forth within the roped-off area while more were stationed to prevent anyone from crossing the barrier.

Grabbing Ellie's arm, he pulled her toward the nearest officer.

"I'm Noel Hathaway, the publisher," he announced, "and I need to get inside."

The officer shook his head. "Sorry, sir, but no one is allowed inside until the fire marshal has assessed the site."

Noel opened his mouth to argue but Ellie interrupted. "I see Jason! He's being treated by one of the EMT teams."

Ellie pushed through the crowd barely apologizing until she reached the back of the ambulance where Jason was being given oxygen while an EMT evaluated his condition.

"Jason! Are you okay?" she gasped out.

Jason smiled weakly and pulled the oxygen mask away from his face. "Yeah, I'm okay. Just got a little too much smoke when I opened the back door. Nothing serious."

"Thank God," Noel murmured from behind Ellie.

The EMT firmly placed the mask back on Jason's face and turned to face them.

"Sorry, he has to keep this on until his lungs are cleared. No talking."

Noel started to protest but at a gentle nudge, looked over his shoulder to see Oscar standing close behind him.

"I'll just go take a peek," Oscar whispered to Noel and Ellie. "They won't even know I was there. I'll be back in a jiffy with a report."

Ellie sighed in relief, then spotted Kirsten and Joe making their way toward them. Kirsten rushed forward and tried to hug Jason.

"Oh, Jason! Are you hurt?" she cried out.

Jason shook his head, then pointed to the mask and shrugged.

"He's being treated for smoke inhalation," Ellie told Kirsten. "That's all we know now."

They turned to look at the newspaper office building. From the front, there didn't appear to be any damage at all, but Ellie knew that, if they could walk around to the back of the building, the story would be quite different. The rear of the Courier building had a central door with a fairly small wooden porch and two low steps. The trash containers were positioned to the right of the door and the rest of the space between the newspaper and the next building offered just enough space four to five cars to park.

Ellie started to walk to her right along the cordoned space to see if she could spot any fire damage along the side of the building. Noel trailed after her. As she reached the point where she could see the side of the building, she signed in relief.

"No obvious fire damage, not even smoke," she murmured.

Behind her Noel let out a breath and whispered, "That's a good sign."

Oscar appeared beside Ellie, causing her to jump slightly.

"Good news," he announced. "The fire was contained to the rear of the building and a small portion of the storage area immediately next to the door. It looked as if Jason was able to grab a fire extinguisher and help keep the fire from spreading into the ceiling or walls inside. But I suspect there will be significant smoke damage."

Ellie groaned. "That means our computers might not be usable. And how much water did they spray into the building? Did they get as far as Jennifer's office? She has all the graphics materials in there."

Ellie replied, "Couldn't you tell?"

Oscar grunted. "It's pretty dark in there, as you well know."

Ellie snapped back, "You can't see in the dark? "Oscar chuckled, "I'm a ghost, not a cat. Maybe we should send Angel in."

Noel put his hand gentlly on her shoulder. "Easy, Ellie. It's going to be okay."

Before Noel could continue, the police chief approached them.

"Just the person I was looking for," he greeted them "Mr. Hathaway, if you would follow me, I have some questions for you. Oh, and round up your staff, whoever is here. Let's walk over to the police station where we can talk privately. Joe, you are not included."

It took minutes to walk the two blocks to the police station where they gathered in a conference room. Ellie took a moment to call Catherine's cell phone, and make sure she and Maybelle were okay.

"We're getting along just famously," Catherine replied. "Don't you worry. We can nap on the sofa and chairs if necessary."

Relieved, Ellie settled into a chair at the oblong table and gazed at the rest of the group. Everyone looked tense. Ellie wondered how much she should tell the police and fire about what they had discovered on their own. Would they ask her to reveal her source? Would they believe their allegations against Matthew Brady? Her mind was spinning with possibilities until she couldn't stand it any more.

"I'm not saying a word," she finally told herself firmly. "Let Noel and the others lead. They have the experience. I'm just a bystander." That made her feel more in control.

Police chief McGrath stepped into the room and closed the door. An expectant hush fell.

"Okay, let's not beat around the bushes here," he began. "Tonight's fire was a blatant attack on the Courier. I know you have been working on finding out who is responsible for this series of fires just as we have. So I have asked you here to respectfully share whatever you might have found out."

Before McGrath could continue, they heard a discrete knock on the door and Jason poked his head around the door frame.

"Okay If I come in?" he asked.

McGrath beckoned Jason in and a nod. Jason crossed the room and chose a chair next to Kirsten.

"First, since Jason has joined us, let's go over what happened tonight," McGrath said.

Jason cleared his throat with a grimace. "I was loading photos onto the system when I thought I smelled smoke. I got up from my workstation and walked through to the rear of the offices. It seemed to be coming from the back end of the building, so I went to the back door and opened it." Jason paused and blinked. It was obvious to Ellie, and probably everyone else, that he was still shook up.

"Flames and smoke blocked the entire door, and the wooden porch was blazing right next to the door. I slammed the door and called 911. Then I ran to bring a fire extinguisher that I knew was stored in the back area and began spraying around the door and the floor. The smoke became too much for me. I dropped the extinguisher and crawled under the smoke to the front where I exited the building."

Jason stopped and sat silent staring down at the top of the conference table.

"Oh, Jason," Kirsten murmured.

McGrath waited for a moment, then continued. "Now we need to discuss why the newspaper was targeted."

Noel spoke up, "We have been gathering as much information as we could on regional fires as well as anything we could find that might indicate who was responsible for these fires. So far, we have one name that seems to meet the criteria for all of the evidence."

McGrath replied, "And that is…" he prompted.

"Matthew Brady," Noel answered. "Brady was released from his job in mid January, and has been in the Creekwood area ever since. Research and interviews indicated that Brady worked as an industrial rep and traveled a great deal. By cross checking his territory with a list of open arson cases, we were able to line up several that coincided with sales trips he was on at the time."

McGrath frowned. "But how did you come to focus on Matthew Brady in the first place."

Dead silence met his question. No one around the table moved or said a word. Ellie felt the pressure and thought carefully about what she felt she could or couldn't say. Finally, she sighed.

"That would be me," she said softly.

McGrath started and turned to face her. "You, Mrs. Franklyn?"

Ellie spoke up. "Yes, sir. A source reached out to me with information that led to our taking a close look at Matthew Brady. A reliable source."

McGrath studied Ellie closely. "And that would be who?"

Ellie responded, "I am afraid I cannot tell you that."

McGrath stared at her for a long moment before asking softly, "And why not?"

Ellie didn't hesitate. "Because I am seriously concerned that if this person's identity becomes known, it will endanger… this person."

McGrath replied, "We can protect the witness."

Ellie immediately stated, "You don't know that. With all due respect, an arsonist like Brady won't care who he hurts if he can stop a person from testifying against him. It's not like a gun or any other kind of weapon. Fires can be lit easily without getting too close. Fire-starting materials can be thrown through windows."

Ellie stopped talking, afraid she wasn't making sense. *What do I know about arsonists?...* she questioned herself. *I'm no expert.*

McGrath gazed at Ellie for a long moment. "I see we are at an impasse here. I will respect your wishes, Mrs. Franklyn. I just hope we can nail down Mr. Brady before anything else goes wrong here."

Noel spoke quickly, "We will do everything we can to help you and your officers find the person responsible for these fires, Chief McGrath. We have a photo record of onlookers at all the fires we have been able to cover in person. If your investigators would like to come to our offices and go through them, they are most welcome."

McGrath nodded. "Thank you, Mr. Hathaway, we will be certain to do that in the next few days, as soon as you have your facility up and running again."

The meeting concluded and Ellie along with her colleagues walked back to where they left their vehicles. Noel drove her home, but declined when she asked if he wanted to come inside for coffee.

"Okay but I do have one question before I go," Ellie said. "Why did you come to my house tonight?"

# CHAPTER 15

Noel's hands gripped the steering wheel tightly. For a moment, Ellie thought he wasn't going to answer her question. Then he slowly lowered his hands and turned to look at her full face.

"I … I wanted to talk to you," he temporized.

"Obviously," Ellie agreed.

Noel made an exasperated sound. "I decided it might be helpful if we were able to just get acquainted more in a place where you felt comfortable. Before you say anything, I knew Maybelle was there. It wasn't like we were going to be alone. Just a casual visit over coffee or tea, general conversation, you know…"

Ellie studied him as he trailed off. He was serious, she decided. But, his timing had been bad, or good depending on how you looked at it. She sighed.

"Okay, I'll accept that," she said. "But in the future, please call first? It wasn't the best timing."

Noel nodded. "And what were Kirsten and Joe doing there?"

"They came over to talk about the arsons and what we could do to convince the police and fire we might have a valid lead," Ellie replied.

Noel laughed, a short snort. "Talk about timing."

Ellie laughed and nodded. "Right. So, now what? I suggest we put personal issues on hold, and work on how we're going to get a newspaper out."

Noel took a deep breath, then nodded again. "Right. I'm going back to the office to find out how long it will be before we can start assessing the damage. I need to call professional cleaners to air out and clean the rear of the building while we have some IT specialists in to evaluate how much damage all the smoke has done to our computer system. I'm going to propose we all meet at the PC for coffee and reconnaissance first thing in the morning…say 8 a.m?"

Ellie reached for the car door handle and nodded in agreement. "See you then," she said over her shoulder. Noel waited until she unlocked the back door before backing out of her driveway. Ellie watched him go with a grim smile on her face. Inside, she found Catherine, her neighbor, and Maybelle snoozing in the living room. Catherine was stretched out on the couch while Maybelle was comfortable wrapped in a quilt and dozing on a recliner.

"Oh, you're back," she heard Catherine murmur as she took off her coat and hung it in a closet next to the front door. "So how bad was it?"

Ellie crossed to the couch where Catherine had drawn her legs up and gazed at the coffee table where the remnants of coffee and cookies held sway. Sitting down in the space Catherine had made, she replied, "Not as bad as it could have been. The entire rear of the newspaper building will have to be replaced but the fire didn't get too far into the storage area."

Catherine nodded wisely. "But the real damage will be from smoke and water," she said. "Exactly, and right now there is no way of assessing how bad it is. We couldn't get inside the building yet. Mr. Hathaway is planning to call in professionals to clean up the mess, and others to evaluate the computer system."

Catherine laughed. "Mr. Hathaway? Oh, Ellie…"

Ellie blushed. "Is it that obvious? I mean, I haven't encouraged him at all but…"

Catherine shook her head. "No, now don't get me wrong. I know it's entirely too soon after dear Jerry's passing. But human feelings don't always pay attention to the demands of social constrictions. Plus, he's such a hunk," she added with a giggle.

"I just can't…" Ellie protested.

Catherine nodded, a more serious expression on her face. "Of course not. And not because of social graces. You need time. You need to fully grieve. You need space. I hope Mr. Hathaway has the grace to accept that. He will if he really cares, you know."

Ellie sighed. "That's exactly what I just told him. And I hope you're right. But now, we need to get some sleep because I have an 8 a.m. meeting to discuss how to put out a paper without an office or computer system. Thank goodness, the printing presses weren't still back there. So… why don't you just stay here if you are comfortable? No need to go out in the cold dark. And Maybelle looks downright at home."

Catherine grinned. "We had the loveliest evening! I wish I had met her years ago. She's quite a gal. And yes, I will happily accept staying until morning. It's the first time I've been out of the house overnight in so long I don't remember the last time."

Upstairs, finally stretched out in bed after what seemed like a year-long day, Ellie found she still couldn't unwind. Vagrant thoughts flitted through her head one after another. Like, how much danger are we all in at home? Did I do the right thing by not exposing my source? Will we be able to get the paper out this week? And finally… what do I do about Noel?

# CHAPTER 16

At a few minutes before 8 a.m., Ellie pushed open the door to the PC, aka the Pinecone Café, and looked around. She spotted some of her coworkers seated in a large, circular booth at the back, and headed for them. Behind her, Jason came in and followed her across the crowded café.

"Good morning," Ellie said as she scrunched into the booth beside Kirsten.

Martha and Jennifer were already there. Jason pressed in beside her. Ellie glanced at Jason's profile and was taken aback at the anger she saw on his youthful face. She laid a gentle hand on his forearm and smiled at him.

"How are you doing, Jason?"

Jason sighed. "I'm so angry I can't even think," he replied through gritted teeth. "I could have been killed or seriously injured last night. How dare someone attack us like that?"

Ellie nodded. "I feel the same way. It's awful to think that a Creekwood resident would do something that cruel."

Before she could continue, Marcie Baker rushed up to the booth, order book in hand.

"What can I bring you to drink," she exclaimed breathlessly. "It's incredibly busy in here, even for a Saturday. I apologize for taking so long to get to you all."

Martha said, "It's not that long, Marcie. Don't fret. I'll have coffee with creamer and one of those marvelous blueberry muffins I saw on the way in."

Jennifer seconded that order. Marcie turned to Ellie with a grin. "The usual?"

Before Ellie could confirm her order, Noel slid into the booth opposite her next to Martha.

"The usual?" he asked with a grin. "How often do you have breakfast here?"

Ellie's expression took on a sad tone. "We used to eat breakfast here almost every Saturday," she explained. "But, it's been a while since…"

Marcie interrupted, "Well, you're here now! One order of cherry almond crepes coming up with lots of coffee and creamer."

"Yum! That sounds wonderful," Kirsten said. "I'll have that, too,"

"And more coffee for me, Marcie," Noel added. "I already ate earlier."

Marcie left, and Noel looked around the booth at his staff. "We're all here. Before we go across the street to the office, let me update you all on where we stand right now. Since the perp didn't enter the building, it has been cleared as a crime scene. Ed is here for the day, directing the professional cleaning crew. We are throwing out all the old paper files that have been stored in the rear of the building as a safety measure. The smoke and ash residue is being cleaned up, and a reconstruction crew is standing by to begin tearing out the fire-damaged walls and porch as soon as the police permit it."

Kirsten frowned. "What about our computers? That smoke could have done a lot of damage."

Noel nodded. "On it. I have a couple of IT people coming in around 9 a.m. to assess the damage and clean out the equipment.

In the meantime, we need to figure out how we are going to put out a paper Wednesday just in case we have major overhaul issues."

Jennifer put in, "If we can network our personal computers with the Courier system, we can work from home until the mess is cleaned up, and we're operational."

Noel smiled at her. "Right, but I am hopeful we will be able to get in without any huge issues. Call me optimistic."

Ellie asked, "So what do we do until the cleanup is complete?"

Noel explained, "The crews will work through the weekend. I am asking all of you to come in early Monday morning to get a running start on what needs to be done to wrap up the Wednesday issue. I know most of you are up to date on stories and that it won't be a tough challenge to finish. I want Jason to take photos of the repair and cleanup so that we can write an upbeat front page store on how the Courier is rising from the ashes, business as usual."

Ellie hoped Noel's optimism was rewarded. As the newspaper team finished their breakfasts and trooped across the street, she nearly held her breath in anticipation of how bad it was going to be. One step into the office's front lobby shocked her, in a totally happy way. In spite of the strong smoke odor and the obvious film of oily smoke residue that coated every surface, the place looked untouched. It looked as if nothing had happened. In the editorial area, Noel's brother, Ed stood in the midst of a bustling yellow-clad clean-up crew of at least half a dozen people. Toward the rear of the building, Ellie could hear Police Chief McGrath and the fire marshal speaking but their words weren't clear. She turned to Noel.

"Okay, Monday morning, 7:30 a.m.? I'll see you all then."

Ellie drove home and parked in her driveway. Janelle's car was parked out on the street.

Inside, she found a cheerful trio sitting around the kitchen table, the aroma of freshly baked cinnamon rolls hanging on the air. Maybelle was perched on a kitchen chair, with Angel curled up on her lap.

"Catherine, thank you so much for staying with Maybelle all this time," Ellie said. "And Janelle, I can't thank you enough for all the help."

Janelle laughed. "No problem. In fact, we may have come to a different solution for keeping Maybelle safe and cared for."

Ellie gaped. "Really? Because I've been worried about having to leave her alone or asking you both to constantly be here for her."

Catherine grinned. "How about we move Maybelle to my house? I'm home all the time. And besides, we have really hit it off. I like the idea of having someone there with me that I can help. I've been alone and feeling useless for too long."

Janelle added, "Yeah, and I can still come over to back Catherine up whenever she needs a break."

Maybelle chimed in, "Yeah, and I get to eat a lot of really great food! Catherine wants to cook for me from all her cookbooks. She claims she hardly cooks for herself at all."

Janelle grinned. "And we will all benefit," she chuckled.

Ellie shook her head ruefully. "It sounds as if you have it all planned out. We should check with Tom Wagner to make sure it meets his approve."

Maybelle burst out laughing. "Oh, poof! We don't need Tom's approval. Let's do this!"

So the next two hours were spend in moving Maybelle from Ellie's home next door to Catherine's. The tough part was physically getting Maybelle there safely. Between the three women, though, it was finally finished.

"Now, Maybelle, do you want Angel with you?" Ellie asked.

"If you don't mind," Maybelle said. "She has been sleeping with me the past few nights, and I'll miss her."

But when Ellie went home to collect the cat and her supplies, the little Siamese was nowhere to be found. She hunted the house from top to bottom without success. Finally, she called Catherine and let them know Angel wouldn't be moving there any time soon.

"That's odd," Ellie thought to herself. "I hope it's not a bad omen."

# CHAPTER 17

"I can't stand it any more!"

Jason dropped into his desk chair and glowered at the computer monitor. Ellie looked up from her keyboard and frowned.

"Can't stand what, Jason?"

Jason slumped back in his chair. "Nothing's happening, that's what. It's been nearly a week since the fire. The police chief keeps asking for more and more photos, but won't share any information, for one thing. And for another..." Jason glanced around the editorial area furtively, then whispered. "There hasn't been another fire."

Kirsten grunted and pushed back from her computer. "Careful, Jason. You might just get exactly what you're asking for."

Before Ellie could add to that sentiment, Noel rounded the corner from his office and gazed around at the three of them.

"First of all, no comment is pretty typical of police departments during investigations," he stated. "And second, I second what Kirsten just said. This community doesn't need another fire."

Ellie sighed. Noel was right. It was frustrating that there didn't seem to be any progress in the police and fire joint investigation. But still, they had been able to put out the weekly edition of the Courier on time, despite being handicapped by the cleanup. The good news had been when the IT experts pronounced their network and computers fully functional without major issues.

"I agree with Jason that it's nerve-racking waiting for something bad to happen," Ellie commented.

Noel nodded. "How is Miss Maybelle handling the move?"

Ellie was relieved at the change in subject. "She's great, and so is Catherine. They've become fast friends. Catherine confessed to me that this was something she really needed, having a friend to help, and it's a relief to me not to worry about leaving Maybelle alone or needing to be home."

Kirsten smiled at Ellie. "That's good to hear. So where did Angel go?"

Ellie frowned. "You know, that was strange. I tried to find her to take over to Catherine's house, but she was nowhere to be found. Sometime that night, I woke to find her sleeping in bed with me. And she definitely doesn't want to go anywhere. When I try to pick her up, she takes off running. Angel has made it clear she wants to stay at my house."

Kirsten grimaced. "I don't know if that's good or bad."

Ellie agreed. "I don't either, but her company is welcome."

Just then, Martha stood up in the front foyer and called over the file cabinets, "Call for Kirsten, line 3."

Kirsten picked up and punched the three button. "Kirsten here," she announced. She listened for a length of time, then asked, "And no one knows where she is? When was she last seen?"

Kirsten listened for several minutes longer while four eager faces waited breathlessly for whatever news she had received. Finally, Kirsten thanked the caller and placed the headset gently down on its base.

"That was Police Chief McGrath. A high school student named Amy Swanson has been reported missing. She went to a friend's house after supper yesterday and was supposed to be back home by 10. When she didn't come home, her parents called the friend and several others Amy hung around with. Then they reported her to the police department."

Ellie tried to keep her shock and fear hidden. Oh, God, she thought, that's Jenny's friend who told her that Matthew Brady was possibly the arsonist. She's been dating Brady's son. This has to be bad news. Ellie looked up to find Noel watching her closely.

"Ellie, please come to my office. Now." He turned and headed for the front office.

Aware that the others two were watching her closely as well, she stood up and followed Noel into his office.

"Please sit down," Noel said, closing the door behind them. He lost no time getting to the point. "Was Amy Swanson your source?"

Ellie shook her head vigorously. "No, but…"

Noel stopped her. "No, don't say anything more. But I'm guessing her name came up in talks with your source, right? Ellie nodded. "And I need to …"

Once again, Noel interrupted. "I understand. Just go. Don't say anything. I'll make sure no one leaves for at least 15 minutes. Will that give you enough time?"

Ellie breathed a sigh of relief. "Yes, it will."

Ellie kept her head down as she went back into the editorial area and gathered up her coat and purse. She quickly left the Courier building and drove to the Atrium where Jenny was most likely to be at this time of day. There were only a few cars in the lot, with lunch long past but supper hour not yet started. She parked her car and took a moment to decide what she was going to do or say, especially if Jenny wasn't available. Pulling a piece of notepaper from her purse, she scribbled a note and folded it into a small square. Then she hurried into the bakery end of the restaurant complex. Spotting Jenny behind the counter, she felt herself relax a bit. A quick glance showed Ellie no one else was in the bakery area.

"Good afternoon, Jenny!" Ellie said cheerfully. "Just the person I wanted to see. I want to pick up three of these luscious scones with the apricot and pecan pieces, if they're available."

Looking closely at Jenny, Ellie realized that she already knew Amy was missing. The teen's eyes were red-rimmed and she was pale.

"Hi, Mrs. Franklyn," Jenny murmured. "You are in luck. We have about a dozen of them left, freshly baked this morning. Let me get them bagged up for you."

Ellie opened her purse and pulled her wallet out. She found a $10 bill and folded it in half with the note inside.

"Perfect!" Ellie responded. "I'm headed home for a tea break, and these will really hit the spot."

Ellie accepted the bag and handed the money to Jenny, who took it to the till. With her back turned to the room, Jenny slipped Ellie's note into her apron pocket and took change from the cash drawer.

"Here you go, Mrs. Franklyn. Enjoy," Jenny said softly.

Ellie left the bakery and walked to her car, looking carefully around her for any lurking figures. No one was in sight, she thought with relief. She drove straight home, wondering when Jenny would find the time and safety to call. Putting the kettle on to heat water for her tea, she pulled one of the scones out of the bag and was shocked to find a folded note tucked between it and another scone.

"Wow, Jenny was hoping I would come," Ellie said to herself. "Smart girl!"

Unfolding the note and reading its contents, Ellie became even more concerned.

"Mrs. Franklyn, Amy was at my house last night. She left around 9:50 so she would be home at 10 but never got there. It's about six blocks, and Amy was riding her bike. I am worried sick about her and scared for myself as well. What can we do?"

Just as she settled back in her kitchen chair to think, her cell phone rang. She barely punched the green talk icon when Jenny's frightened voice blurted out, "Did you find my note?"

Ellie replied, "Yes, I did. And I am very worried about your safety as well as Amy's. My first thought is where can you go that's safe for you?"

Jenny said, "I told my parents everything. They know now what Amy told me about Mr. Brady and how he's been really creepy whenever she spends time with his son."

Ellie sighed. "Good, they needed to know, and so do the police. Did you talk to them yet?"

Jenny groaned. "No, not yet but I'm sure my parents are planning to do that. I'm scared."

Ellie sighed. "You should be. Perhaps you need to all get away for a while until this is resolved."

"But, the restaurant!" Jenny cried. "We can't just close it up. We have dozens of reservations and party events booked. My parents can't afford to close down and pass up all that revenue. Yes, I know what you want to say, that people will understand. But will they, really?"

Ellie thought for a moment. "Is there enough staff to keep it open, with your parents managing it from a distance?"

Jenny said, "Possibly. Most of the wait staff is experienced and have been very good when my parents have needed to be out of town for a day or two… that's an option."

Ellie added, "Jenny, do you have any clue where Mr. Brady would have taken Amy?"

"Not at all," Jenny replied. "He has to be hiding her somewhere no one would look."

Ellie continued, "Think about it. Call my cell anytime day or night if you have an idea. We need to save her and put Mr. Brady behind bars where he belongs."

# CHAPTER 18

Ellie was up and dressed almost before the sun rose the next morning. Dressed in comfortable jeans and a gray sweatshirt, she came downstairs and hurried to the kitchen where she started her two-mug coffee brewer. Then she opened the refrigerator in an effort to decide what to eat for breakfast.

"An omelet," she told herself, "with cheese, diced green onion and some of the smoky ham left over from Christmas."

She broke two eggs into a bowl and dug through a drawer looking for the smaller of her two whisks. Instead, she pulled out an item lying beside them with a frown.

"What the heck?" she muttered, gazing down at Jerry's Swiss army knife. "What's that doing in here? I don't remember putting it there and I'm certain Jerry didn't."

Absent-mindedly, she put the knife in her front jeans pocket with a reminder to give it to one of her sons. Then she whisked the eggs and put a small frying pan on the stove to preheat. Ellie pulled the ham she had diced and bagged from the freezer, plus the rest of the ingredients for the omelet and a loaf of thick-sliced farmhouse bread.

As breakfast started cooking, Ellie thought about what needed to be done at work in the Courier office that morning, along with whatever errands she could run later. She decided to eat at the PC as a treat and not pack a lunch.

Instead, she pulled a list pad from its drawer and started lining up what she hoped to accomplish.

"Let's see... today's Thursday, so I need to get the PSAs updated and the event notifications keyed in first. Then I can copy-edit any stories that are already in. And after work, I need to buy more postage stamps, stop at the library for something to read and check in on Catherine and Maybelle."

Less than an hour later, Ellie pulled up in front of the Creekwood Courier office ready to work. The morning went quickly. Last to be worked on was Jason's pictorial rehash of the arson investigation, with a collage of photos covering every fire. At the back of her mind, she kept wondering where the arsonist might have taken Amy Swanson.

"It's not like there's a lot of empty buildings in town, and he's not likely to have her at his house," she mused.

Wrapping up her morning's work, Ellie put her jacket on, grabbed her purse and went out through the front office, saying goodbye to Martha who was sorting mail.

"Martha, I'm going to lunch, and then I'll be back to finish inputting whatever we got in today's mail. See you in a bit."

Martha nodded absently, barely looking up as she focused on the pile of mail in front of her.

Across the street at the PC, Ellie found a small booth at the back of the restaurant and ordered one of her favorite lunches, mac and cheese with chunks of crab meat in a Rangoon-type sauce. Marcie, the waitress, kidded her about it being "kid food" but Ellie didn't mind… it was delicious. She was half-way through the generous bowl of pasta when something she had just seen in Jason's photos clicked.

"Of course, we need to check out the old farmhouse where those two barns burned down last winter," she realized. "I'll bet no one even gave it a thought and it would be perfect. Besides, the arsonist certainly knows about it."

By the time Ellie finished lunch, she had decided to drive out there and check it out, just take a look and see if anyone had been around. Besides, it was a lovely day and she had plenty of time to finish the PSAs Friday morning. Without thinking, she went straight to her car and began the 10-minute drive out into the wooded countryside where the old farmstead was located. In seemingly no time, she was pulling into the old, rutted drive that led to the ram-shackle old house.

Ellie stepped out of her car and took a slow, careful look around. She wasn't sure but it seemed like there were tire tracks that appeared relatively fresh, with broken dried weeds and grass indicating traffic. It was so quiet, no wind and hardly a birdcall. Ellie shivered a bit in the early spring chill and took a tentative step toward the hulking two-story stone house.

"Just a quick look around the house," she told herself. "I can peek in the windows."

Carefully, she locked the car with her purse inside, and walked to the wooden porch with its sagging steps. They creaked when she put her weight on them. She tiptoed across the porch and peered into the front door through its glass window. Just a long, dark hallway with a living room opening to the right. Out of curiosity, she tried the front door.

"It's unlocked," she whispered.

Before she could change her mind, Ellie opened the weather-beaten door slowly and stepped inside. A few steps allowed her to see most of the living room, empty except for scattered pieces of lumber, dust and cobwebs. To her left was another door that opened into what looked like an old-fashioned parlor. Ahead was a staircase that rose up the living room's back wall to the second floor.

"No way I'm going up there," Ellie murmured.

Ellie moved carefully toward the rear of the house through the living room and into a long, narrow area that might have once been the dining room. No furniture remained but what might have been the base of a chandelier was centered in the dingy ceiling. Ellie continued on toward what she imagined would be the kitchen. She stepped inside and gasped.

Tied to a decrepit, spindly kitchen chair was a young woman. Her hands were bound to the chair's arms, and her legs were tied to the chair's legs. She had a gag tied tightly around her head, covering her mouth. Barely more than a teenager, the young woman had to be Amy Swanson.

Ellie rushed to her side and fumbled around with the knots on the gag until she was able to loosen them enough to remove it. Before she could say a word, they both heard the sound of a car pulling up and a door slamming.

"Oh, my God! He's back!" Amy screamed at Ellie. "We have to get out of here!"

Ellie felt her pockets for her cell phone and realized she had locked it in the car with her purse. But her hand hit something hard in the front pocket of her jeans, and she pulled out the Swiss army knife. Frantically, she began sawing at the ropes. Glancing over her shoulder, Ellie caught sight of a large man getting out of a car and staring at her car through the front window. Then he looked toward the house.

"Hurry, please!"

Ellie resumed trying to cut the tough ropes while listening for any sounds that indicated the man was coming inside the house. Just as the rope holding Amy's hands to the chair broke through, they heard the sound of glass breaking and a horrendous "WHOOSH!"

Fire exploded across the wooden living floor in a wave as a bottle filled with some kind of flammable fluid burst. They could already feel the heat. Ellie began rapidly trying to cut the ties around Amy's feet so she could get up. Her hands were still tied together.

WHOSH! Glass breaking in the kitchen, followed by another firebomb, put Ellie and Amy in critical danger immediately. Both doorways out of the farmhouse were now blocked by a fierce fire that roared as it engulfed the house at an unbelievable rate.

Ellie glanced up at the dining room window at the glass. Across the space, just inside the living room archway, was a three-foot-long piece of half-rotted two-by-four. Ellie gave the knife to Amy and screamed, "Keep cutting!"

The fire was inching close at incredible speed. "Can I?" Ellie wondered, then decided, "Yes, I can."

She stood up and immediately was inundated with acrid smoke. Bending over and staying low, Ellie wobbled across the floor and grabbed the board. Keeping low, she returned to Amy, who had managed to cut through the ropes binding her feet. Ellie helped her up and ran to the dining room window. She swung the two-by-four as hard as she could at the window, which shattered into a thousand pieces. Ellie beat on the window frame to remove the shards of glass sticking up treacherously from its base.

"Come on, Amy, climb through!" she yelled.

A deep, threatening voice stopped them.

"Not so fast," Matthew Brady warned them, holding a pistol pointed directly at Amy.

# CHAPTER 19

Noel breezed into the Creekwood Courier office and stopped at Martha's desk.

"So where is everyone?" he asked, glancing at his watch.

Martha looked up from her monitor. "Kirsten is coordinating the story with the fire department, and Jason is covering the track meet at the high school."

Noel frowned and looked over the filing cabinets behind Martha. "Where's Ellie?"

Martha started. "Gosh, she went to lunch but said she would be back to finish the new PSAs. She must have changed her mind," Martha stuttered.

Noel turned around and went back to the front door, where he leaned partway out. He studied all the cars which were angle-parked along the Main.

"No sign of her car," Noel commented, coming back into the office with a disappointed look on his face. "I'll be in my office for the next hour or so. Send any calls in to me."

Noel slipped behind his desk and logged into his computer. But before he could do anything else, a familiar voice interrupted him.

"Noel! Ellie is in trouble. She needs help right away!" the ghost of Oscar Maywood whispered urgently.

"What! Where? Why?" Noel demanded, standing up again and glaring at Oscar.

Oscar continued, "She drove out to the old farmhouse where those fires were in January to see if Amy Swanson might be out there. She found Amy, but Matthew Brady found them. You have to get help right away!"

Noel dashed out of his office. "Martha! Call 911! Send the police and fire departments out to the old farmstead. Ellie's out there and in trouble."

Before Martha could say a word, Noel rushed out of the door and ran to his car. He piled in and started it up, revving out of his parking space and heading out of town at a high rate of speed. Hoping against hope, he sped through the countryside on two-lane roads not meant for speed.

"Damn it, I told her to be careful," Noel muttered to himself.

Meanwhile, Ellie and Amy faced a grim Matthew Brady whose gun hand never wavered.

"You can't leave us in here to burn up," Ellie pleaded.

"Yes, I can, and I'm going to," Brady replied. "No one told you to meddle in my business."

Ellie growled, "Your business? You mean burning down other people's property and killing little girls?"

Amy chirped in, "Yeah, what's the matter with you, anyway?"

Brady burst out in a brutal sound that might have been laughter. "That's none of your business as well, nosy little snip. You should have left well enough alone."

Amy yelled back, "Your wife told Brian and me to get something out of the car. When we couldn't find it inside the car, Brian looked in the trunk and found all that fire-starting stuff. It's your fault that you had it there."

Brady smirked. "Well, it's your problem now, isn't it?"

Behind Ellie and Amy, the heat was becoming intolerable. Almost unbearable smoke had formed a dense cloud over their heads that hung lower and lower every second. Ellie dropped down on her knees and moved closer to the window to get some fresh air. Amy followed her lead.

Brady waved his gun and shouted, "Stand up! I want to be able to see you at all times. Don't try to sneak out another way."

A groan of creaking timbers and a drift of cinders warned them the roof was engulfed and ready to collapse. To Ellie, there didn't seem any way they could escape. Fire blazed in both the kitchen and living rooms. There was no way they could crawl through it to the little parlor. Ellie started coughing, and Amy was choking on the smoke. Both were brushing embers off of their clothes and out of their hair constantly.

"That's it," Ellie finally shouted. "I'm getting out of here!"

She had just started to make a move toward the window when someone crashed into Brady, throwing him onto the ground.

It was Noel! Ellie gasped. Where did he come from, she briefly wondered before grabbing Amy's arm and pulling her to the window.

"Quick, get out now!" she said, shoving Amy halfway through the broken-out frame.

Amy didn't hesitate. She dove through the window, then turned to help Ellie escape the flames.

Ellie reached down, grabbed the two-by-four, and lunged through the window, helped by a strong tug from Amy.

"Run!" Ellie yelled at her, then looked around to where Noel and Brady were fighting for the gun on the ground a few feet away. Before she could react, Brady punched Noel in the throat, breaking his hold on Brady's jacket. In a flash, Brady gained control of the gun and stood up, pointing it down at Noel with a vicious snarl.

"You just had to interfere," Brady growled. "You've made a fatal mistake."

Ellie gripped the two-by-four firmly and ran at Brady. She stopped long enough to take a mighty swing at him. The board connected with the side of Brady's head, and he dropped like a stone. The gun fell out of his hand. Noel grabbed it and scuttled backward before standing up. The two stood there over Brady's prone body, staring at each other.

Noel snorted. "Nice swing," he said.

Ellie rolled her eyes and groaned.

Behind them, the welcome sound of sirens filled the still air. Police squads and fire trucks began pulling into the area around the burning farmhouse, not a moment too soon. With a thunderous roar, the roof collapsed into the house, sending flames, sparks and smoke billowing into the sky.

An EMT approached Ellie and asked, "Are you okay?"

Ellie took quick stock of herself. "Just some cuts and probably a lot of bruises," she replied.

"What happened to him?" the EMT said, pointing to Brady lying on the ground.

Ellie shrugged. "I hit him in the head with this," she answered, showing him the two-by-four with a glob of blood and hair attached.

"Whoa!" he responded before going to the prone man's side and stooping down to check on him.

"He's alive, probably has a concussion."

"Probably," Amy quipped. "Serves him right."

Several other EMTs joined him as they started working on Brady. One went to get a gurney from the ambulance. The firefighters unrolled the hose and connected it to a water tanker truck that rolled into place beside their truck. But there was little anyone could do to save the old farmhouse that had stood for decades on the Wisconsin farmland. It was going to be a total loss.

"So, what happened here?"

Ellie started violently. She hadn't noticed Police Chief McGrath coming to talk to her.

"It's a long story, chief," she said. "Am I in trouble?"

McGrath studied her worried expression. "I doubt it. I mean, I don't know exactly what transpired here, but I'm fairly certain you acted out of self-defense."

Amy walked up to them. "More than that, much more," she stated. "Ellie found me when no one else knew where to look. She saved my life. She saved Mr. Hathaway's life when Brady pointed his gun at him and threatened to shoot him. Mrs. Franklyn took him out like a pro."

Ellie felt the blush radiating from her face.

Looking past McGrath, Ellie saw Kirsten and Jason climbing out of Kirsten's car and running over. Jason immediately pulled his camera out of his carrying case and began shooting photos of the spectacular fire, which was beginning to dampen down. Kirsten looked from Ellie to Noel to McGrath and grinned.

"Something tells me we're going to have one heck of a great front page next week," Kirsten commented.

Before Ellie could respond, an EMT approached her and asked if she needed treatment. Ellie realized that her throat was raw from the smoke, her eyes were watery and burning, and there were several painful areas on her arms and legs. Looking down, she could see rips through her jeans where glass shards in the smashed window had cut through to her skin. There were more on her arms below the elbows.

"Come with me," the EMT said as she gently took hold of Ellie's wrist. "We'll get you checked out."

Ellie didn't notice Noel following as she allowed herself to be led to the second ambulance. The other ambulance was already leaving, carrying Brady to the hospital in Madison. As the EMT checked her over and treated each cut, Ellie stared wistfully at the fire.

"What?" Noel asked.

"My late husband's Swiss army knife," Ellie said softly. "I found it in a kitchen drawer this morning and, for some reason, stuck it in my pocket. Thank goodness I did. It was what saved Amy's life. I was able to cut the ropes in time to get her out. And now it's in there," she added with a nod of her head toward the fire.

She looked at Noel with such a woebegone expression that he didn't have the heart to chew her out for not telling Martha where she was going. Not yet, anyway, he vowed. Instead, he gently pushed a strand of hair away from her eyes. He sighed deeply.

"I'm sorry you lost that knife," Noel began. "But you had it when it counted most. Amy Swanson is alive and safe, thanks to you. But how on earth did you figure out where she was?"

Ellie thought back to the PC lunch. "I was thinking about the photo layout Jason is working on, and at the same time, wondering where there was an empty building that Brady could hold Amy in. It just suddenly clicked."

Noel was impressed. "Good instincts," he murmured. "I think you missed your calling."

Ellie grunted. "I don't know… the high school attendance office could be pretty daunting."

Noel burst out laughing, and Ellie almost cracked a smile.

"The question is, what's next?" she continued. "I know Brady will be arrested and charged. But what about me? I don't want to whine, but I did clobber him hard. What if he dies?"

Noel wanted to reassure her, but he had to admit to himself that it might be a "gray area." Instead, he helped her to her feet and said, "Let's just get you home for now. Worry about the fallout tomorrow."

# CHAPTER 20

Ellie drove home through the twilight alone. She had refused to allow Noel or anyone else to either drive her home or follow her. All she wanted to do was go home and be alone. The need to be home was overwhelming. It was her fortress, her refuge. She didn't want to talk over what happened, not right then. All she wanted was a hot mug of tea and solitude.

Angel met her at the door, wrapping her sinewy length around Ellie's legs. While Ellie heated water for a pot of tea, Angel kept watch curled in front of the stove on her rug. Ellie put the teapot, cream, a mug and teaspoon, and a blueberry muffin on a small tray and carried it into the living room, where she set it on a side table. Then she dropped down into her recliner and propped her feet up. Angel leaped up and settled in her lap, purring gently.

Sighing deeply, Ellie began going over her day minute by minute. Everything was okay until she had that brilliant idea to investigate the old farmhouse. That's where the trouble started. And she realized the mistakes she had made. Not telling Martha where she was going was the worst one. Leaving her cell phone in the car was another. Going into the house after telling herself she wouldn't. She should have spotted Amy from a window and called the police.

"But then, I would have been outside and vulnerable when Brady showed up," she told herself. "I bet I would have ended up tied to the other end of the chair. So, what did I do right?"

That was harder to see, Ellie realized. Yes, she had found Amy. Yes, she had cut her free with the knife that Jerry had somehow left in that drawer. And now, she couldn't even remember what she had been looking for when she found it or why she had put it in her pocket. Thank goodness she had, she realized.

Ellie heard a soft knock on the front door.

"Darn it, I told them to leave me alone," she muttered, moving the cat off her lap and setting her mug aside.

But when she opened the door, ready to defend her need to be alone, she found her good friend Janelle standing there. Ellie opened the door, and without a moment's hesitation, stepped into the open arms Janelle offered. Ellie burst into tears, and her knees sagged.

"My goodness, Ellie," Janelle said. "I've heard all kinds of stories. Tell me what really happened."

Janelle guided Ellie back into the living room, where they both sank down on the sofa. For several moments, Ellie couldn't talk.

Janelle rubbed her back and murmured, "Just cry it all out. You'll feel better."

Finally, her sobbing subsided. Janelle handed her another tissue and waited patiently.

"I really screwed up," Ellie sputtered.

Janelle shook her head. "That's not what I heard," Janelle told her. "I heard you are the heroine of the day, finding Amy Swanson, saving both her's and Noel's lives, and taking Matthew Brady down all before the police and fire arrived."

Ellie snorted. "If I had used some common sense, none of that would have happened."

Janelle laughed. "Oh, really? What would have?"

Ellie began, "Well, if I had stayed outside and called it into the police department…"

Janelle interrupted, "You would have been outside when Brady arrived with a gun. Amy would still have been trapped inside. Probably both of you would be dead now."

Ellie sat there stunned. "But, but…"

Janelle said firmly, "No buts. You did really well. Perhaps not perfect, but good. It all ended right."

Ellie sniffed. "What if Brady dies? Will they charge me with manslaughter?"

Janelle shook her head. "Not likely. You not only acted in self-defense but also saved two lives. I don't think the authorities will be in a hurry to accuse you of anything."

Ellie felt herself relaxing slightly. Maybe it was going to be okay. Janelle stayed a bit longer, then reluctantly left after Ellie assured her she would be alright. Almost immediately, Ellie's cell phone rang.

"Hello, Susan," Ellie answered, recognizing the number displayed as her daughter.

"Mom! What in the hell were you thinking?" Susan exploded. "It's all over the news from Chicago, Milwaukee, and Madison, and I wouldn't be surprised if it went national."

Ellie sighed. "I'm okay," she assured Susan. "Just a few scrapes and bruises."

Susan wasn't mollified. "You told me you were writing features and copy editing… in the office. How about you stay in the office and let other people be heroic?"

Ellie shook her head. "Susan, the arsonist set fire to the Courier office last week. Jason was in the building. You can't escape from criminals."

Susan was quiet for a moment. "Okay, I get it. But can't you go back to work for the school district?"

Ellie laughed ruefully. "No, but do you want to know something I just realized? I really like working on the paper. I like the people I work with. They are hard-working, talented, committed, and honest. I like feeling like I'm doing something to help keep the community informed and cohesive. Besides, how often do you think something like this is going to happen?"

"Never would be my hope," Susan retorted. "But honestly, I suppose this isn't something you'd expect to happen in a small town like Creekwood."

Ellie replied, "Exactly, which is why I'm going to continue working there. I do promise I won't take off without letting someone know where I'm going, and I doubt I'll ever do it alone again."

It was Susan's turn to sigh. "Okay, if you promise. The boys are upset. They didn't call because they were afraid they'd blow their tops."

Ellie grimaced. "I promise. I learned a few things today. Oh, and something weird happened. Do you remember Dad's Swiss army knife?"

Susan said, "Yes, I do. He carried it around all the time and kept it razor sharp."

Ellie told Susan what had happened that morning when she found the knife, and Susan gasped.

"Oh, my goodness! Someone was watching over you for certain," Susan exclaimed.

Ellie didn't mention Oscar, who had also been watching over her. Noel had told her that Oscar had warned him about the situation Ellie and Amy were facing in time to arrive and help save them. Throwing a ghost into the story would not help matters, Ellie decided.

After a restless night, Ellie was up with the sun the next morning. She was sitting at the kitchen table sipping coffee and working on a list of things she wanted to accomplish when a familiar voice interrupted.

"Good morning, Ellie," Oscar said, startling her enough to almost spill her coffee.

"Merrrrowww," Angel greeted Oscar from her rug in front of the stove.

"Oh, Oscar!" Ellie exclaimed.

"Sorry about that, my dear," Oscar smiled urbanely. "I haven't quite got the gist of popping in on folks unannounced yet. Anyway, I dropped by to see how you are."

"I'm fine, thanks to you," Ellie replied. "Noel told me how you warned him that I needed help. It's because of you that he arrived in time to save Amy and me."

Oscar beamed. "You are very welcome, Ellie. I wanted to let you know that now things are settled down and you are safe, you probably won't be seeing me."

"Oh, I'm sorry to hear that," Ellie said. "What are you going to do?"

Oscar smiled even more widely. "I'll be keeping an eye on Maybelle, of course. Can't desert my favorite friend. Oh, by the way, Catherine and Maybelle have decided that even when the nursing home is rebuilt, they will stay together. Such a wonderful friendship! It's exactly what they both needed."

Ellie frowned. "How is that going to work out?"

Oscar replied, "Catherine has a bedroom on the first floor all fixed up, and they have made arrangements for a visiting nurse to drop in a couple of times weekly to check on her."

Ellie smiled. "That sounds perfect. But what about you?"

Oscar airily announced, "Oh, I'll be around just in case."

And with that, he faded away.

Ellie was a bit nervous as she entered the front door of the Creekwood Courier that morning. Not sure how her co-workers would greet her; she felt they might be put out or upset. But Martha greeted her with a huge grin.

"Here she is, the Creekwood celebrity!" Martha proclaimed. "You have been getting dozens of phone calls from residents wanting to thank you and curious about exactly what happened, of course."

Ellie grimaced. "I can imagine," she replied. "Ahhh, is everyone here?"

Martha nodded. "Noel wants a meeting with all hands on deck at 8:30."

Ellie felt a frisson that alternated between expectation and apprehension. She eyed the closed door to Noel's office before going to her desk. She slipped into her chair and immediately logged onto her computer. Kirsten leaned over and raised her hand high, asking for a high five.

"Good going, Ellie!" Kirsten said. "Jason and I worked late last night and have the frontpage coverage of the farmhouse fire nearly wrapped up. The only thing left is your interview."

Ellie was aghast. "My interview?"

Kirsten grinned. "Yup. You are the heroine of the piece. We can't hardly publish a story like this without including your point of view. After all, you saved Amy and Noel and decked Brady."

Ellie snorted. "Are you going to include all the mistakes I made?"

Kirsten replied, "What? You made two small mistakes. You didn't tell anyone where you were going and you locked your phone in your car. Otherwise, you did absolutely great. And wait until you see Jason's photos! They are magnificent!"

Before Kirsten could continue, Noel swept out of his office and joined them in the editorial area.

"We're all here, great! Let's get started on the next issue," Noel said without preamble. "How does the frontpage look, Kirsten?"

Kirsten checked her notes. "All done except for Ellie's part. Jason took awesome photos. And Jennifer has a preliminary layout ready for approval."

Noel replied, "Good job, Jason! I can't wait until I see what you have contributed. And, ah, Ellie? I'll be copy-editing this one because you are included in the story."

Ellie realized that this was the ethical way to handle it. Otherwise, she would have been tempted to edit much of her interview out. She nodded in agreement.

"You'll be relieved to know that Matthew Brady will recover from his… err, head wound," Noel added with a smirk. "He has a massive concussion, but it's not expected to be fatal. He is being transferred to UW Wisconsin Hospital in Madison for advanced treatment, after which he will be formally charged with multiple counts of arson and one count of homicide."

Ellie breathed a sigh of relief. It didn't sound like Brady would be free any time soon.

Noel continued, "Other than that, we have the usual coverage to sandwich into the paper. I know you all don't need me to tell you how much I appreciate how hard you've worked to make this paper work."

And with that final statement, Noel rose and returned to his office. Ellie settled into her chair and pulled the file folder of PSAs in front of her. Back to normal, she thought, and it felt good. By noon, she was ready for a break. Kirsten was, too. Jason was out on assignment and Jennifer was still putting the finishing touches on the front-page final layout.

"Hey, Kirsten, want to grab lunch at the PC?" Ellie asked.

"I thought you'd never ask," Kirsten quipped, rising from her chair and logging off.

Ellie did the same. As she and Kirsten passed Noel's open office door, he called out to her.

"I'll be with you in a sec," Ellie said, and reluctantly turned to enter Noel's office.

Noel leaned back in his chair and indicated that Ellie should take a seat. But she shook her head and said Kirsten was waiting for her.

"I was hoping to have a word with you," Noel said, clearly disappointed. "But I just want you to know that I believe you did a superb job. Don't beat yourself up on any little mistakes. And also," he hesitated, then went on resolutely, "I was hoping we could get together later on today or maybe tomorrow for dinner."

Ellie stood in the doorway and gazed at him. "I … not yet. It's been less than six months. Please."

Noel sighed, and his shoulders sagged. "Okay, but tell me if I have any chance at all."

Ellie smiled slightly. "There's always a chance, Noel," she whispered.

**THE END**

Milton Keynes UK
Ingram Content Group UK Ltd.
UKHW021200251124
451300UK00025B/282